D1056033

*Book of Wings*

# *Book*

## *of*

# *Wings*

A NOVEL

## Tawhida Tanya Evanson

ESPLANADE BOOKS

THE FICTION IMPRINT AT VÉHICULE PRESS

ESPLANADE BOOKS IS THE FICTION IMPRINT AT VÉHICULE PRESS

Published with the generous assistance of the Canada Council for
the Arts, the Canada Book Fund of the Department of Canadian
Heritage, and the Société de développement des entreprises culturelles
du Québec (SODEC).

Canadä **SODEC** Québec

Canada Council    Conseil des arts
for the Arts        du Canada

This is a work of fiction. Any resemblance to people or events is
coincidental and unintended by the author.

Esplanade Books editor: Dimitri Nasrallah
Cover design: David Drummond
Typeset in Minion and MrsEaves
Printed by Marquis Imprimeur

LIBRARY AND ARCHIVES CANADA CATALOGUING IN PUBLICATION

Title: Book of wings : a novel / Tawhida Tanya Evanson.
Names: Evanson, Tanya, 1972- author.
Identifiers: Canadiana (print) 20200391976 | Canadiana (ebook)
20200405128 | ISBN 9781550655643
(SOFTCOVER) | ISBN 9781550655704 (EPUB)
Subjects: LCGFT: Novels.
Classification: LCC PS8559.V377 B66 2021 | DDC C813/.6—dc23

Published by Véhicule Press, Montréal, Québec, Canada

Distribution by LitDistCo
www.litdistco.ca
Printed in Canada on FSC certified paper.

*for the Beloved*

# Some Words and Phrases

| | |
|---|---|
| *As-salamu alaykum* | Peace be upon you |
| *Astaghfirullah* | I ask forgiveness |
| *Azan* | Muslim call to prayer |
| *Café cassé au Paradis* | Broken coffee in Paradise |
| *Eyvallah* | I accept |
| *Hamdullah* | Praise God |
| *Inshallah* | God-willing |
| *La ilaha illallah* | There is no God but God |
| *Les épées empoisonnées* | The poisoned swords |
| *Mais épanouie* | But fulfilled |
| *Mashallah* | What God has willed, May it continue |
| *Murshid* | Guide or teacher |
| *Nur* | Divine Light |
| *Nurun ala Nur* | Light upon Light |
| *Quel instinct pourri* | What rotten instinct |
| *Semazenbashi* | Head of the whirling dervishes |
| *Zikr* | The practice of divine remembrance |

# One

I died from inanimate and became animate
I died from animate and became animal
I died from animality and became human
Why should I be afraid
When have I ever become less by dying?

–Hz. Mevlana Jalálu'ddín Rúmí
MATHNAWÍ BOOK III 3901

## Paris in the Springtime

TODAY I LEFT MY LOVER for a room with a view. He had trouble managing his time travel with me. It took only a few days for him to pack up and sail on—two wings, *un oiseau*. He was careful, came with intention but left no seed. We dive like birds, even into shit.

Outside the window, pigeons picked at invisible morsels on rue St-Jacques. Invasion took flight. Overcast sky that morning in the Latin Quarter. I took unsettled steps down the steep, winding, velvet staircase at l'Hôtel de Médicis without ever looking back. How could I? My heart lay burst on the horizon, a red ocean hemorrhage; it was Paris in the springtime.

Did he think I would remain under such conditions? On our final night I chose to sleep on the wooden floor of our dusty room, waiting for daylight, waiting for the descent into Hell. I listened for Guan or Hausa voices to come save me, prayers of redemption, otherworldly African women to chant around my tomb. All I got were the heated moans of a woman making love in a nearby room.

My vulva pulsed. I touched myself when Shams went out that morning before the flood. I hadn't finished by the time he returned and resented him for it. In his outstretched hands, a bouquet of roses the colour of cowardice—as if this would lift my spirits beyond our departures.

In a blunt second, Shams had aged a decade. Barely twenty-nine with wrinkles on the forehead now pronounced, a furrowed brow of doubt, the face of a guilt complex. There was no concealing a human being in supplication for falling out of love. Who knows how the heart moves, until it stops moving toward you. I did not see it coming. What do you do when the object of your love disappears in plain sight? Love lifts and is itself, a veil, said a voice from the other side of the story. This is the difference between rose-coloured and a hit of direct sun.

Shams left for a moment to use the bathroom in the hall and I finished myself off outside of him quick, deep, for the first time without him in over a year—my own unfamiliar finger between the legs.

In the end, I left the room because so little of him was still in it. The only part that mattered had disappeared. I left the roses behind because *l'odeur de la mort était insupportable*. Walked out into the cloudy fifth arrondissement. An early April morning, 2002. There are three versions of this story: mine, his and the Truth.

# Sorrow and Ceremony

I TOOK A SEA-GREEN LEATHER seat in a far corner of La Contrescarpe and ordered red. The tavern was empty except for a fashionable French couple dipping toast points into duck liver pâté, quietly bored with each other. In the corner by the tall bookcases, a Black Christian monk in full white tunic and brown scapular robes sat with coffee, reading *Le Monde* like nothing. His cinnamon skin glowed in the orange afternoon sun, he was draped in layers, wood-rosaried at the hip, wrist, and shoulder. He suddenly burst out laughing with his whole body. All our heads gunned. He caught himself quick, returned to calm, assiduous prayer. A vow of silence, folded hands. Folded newspaper, smooth syrupy fingers, nails pink and lustrous. The shine of melanin. Our eyes met and he smiled wide. Solidarity says, "Smile, sister, this too shall pass."

I bowed my head in his direction, put my hand to heart, but I am not comfortable. This calm is a public exterior.

I am ill. I cannot hug this road alone, operate the device with any real accuracy. The tentacles aren't connected to me. Aren't my own.

*"Monsieur! Un autre verre, j'vous prie. Il me faut la tête chaude avant le coucher du soleil."* Sir! Another glass, please. I need my head hot before the sun sets.

When hiding in the shadows, smoke is a natural shield. I tried in vain to bring up the image of greying skin, cracked cheeks concave as they sucked on a cigarette, creases remaining long after inhalation, ashes embedded in skin. This did nothing to detract me. The old habit returned with ease and I took up smoking like an old lover.

Near the end of our affair, Shams would not even let me into his mouth. Lips closed at the nearing, legs shut, eyes on some upward vanishing point. I smashed a left shin into the corner of the bed one afternoon. It crippled me for a moment he did not react to. The scar remains to this day. Bone-deep but only a tinted scratch on the surface at the time. Airborne oil. A heavy leak. Ours were not real actions anymore, they were transactions.

The dry grape filled my head after only four sips. I sat calm in the corner, trying for a low profile. It had only been a few days since Shams had flown, though his body remained nearby. I could feel it.

I walked out of the bar after four glasses, if only to retain my public dignity. Now I'm drunk on the wine of my own making. Ha! But to uncork devotion simply through the tempered wails of the newborn, celibate, wedded to prophets. O Ancestors, where are your ceremonies? Please, I need them now.

# Dream Fist

THAT NIGHT IN THE DREAM I had a meeting with a man. He was waiting for me at the wrong place, standing in ruins under high Corinthian columns. Taking my hand, we entered the ancient city network. Was it Alexandria or Pergamum?

Walking the stone capital at night, it began to rain. Unknown insects fell to the ground. Snow fell in with the insects. I ask my friend what the dream means. She tells me it is a wet dream.

I arrived at the Great Library and it began to rain scarabs. I picked one up from the snowy ground and removed its carapace, licked its inner meat. Shams says that this dream is of things coming to an end.

"I know better," I say. "Even when you sense apocalypse, pluck some of it off the ground and feast."

# The Disappearance of the
# Disappearance

I WANT FREEDOM. Freedom from following. I advise you, my wrath is strong. It is rhythmic smoke from my nostrils, lightning from my hands, twice. It controls the degree of lust in the glance of a silver-haired French father holding his child on rue Soufflot. He blushes. Brushes my shoulder walking past, past the Panthéon of the deads where the living pay silver to visit stone. Here, take my pelvis, you rock, a dying response to Love. These movements are not engineered, they are reactive.

I am I, we shall not change me. A minor improvement in the document perhaps, an amendment to the law. My methods of escape include road, water, air and direct death; Shams' method required no movement at all. He just stood there. No one can touch me now. I pound at the heart of my own wound. This is a forward disowning of the body. I take off my clothes and reveal it.

"Look for the Beloved," said Shams, turning away from me.

Now I will tell my people about the man who left me for a stick of bamboo. Ha! I left him for the mother of all Africa. But this was not a time for war. I had brought him to paradise and he left me there. Next time, I won't bring anyone so close to the water, if they are still learning to swim and I, to drown. If you see me with arms flailing about, DO NOT SAVE ME. I am flying away.

# Two

Birds lift into the air
expecting to be safe

–Baha'uddin Walad
AL-MA'ARIF, THE DROWNED BOOK II 2:13-14

## Via Purgativa

SHE WAS A CUTTER RIG NAMED *My Jo*. A single mast sailboat marooned at Marina Paraíso on Isla Mujeres off the edge of Mayan Mexico. It was March, only one month earlier, when Shams and I had been looking to work for passage—anywhere. The boat had a broken autopilot and a captain named Charlie on the hunt for two things: an open weather window and an easygoing crew to help motor up to Jacksonville. Shams and I came on board and all the elements fell into place. Captain Charlie and his hound dog Sirius invited first mates Gabrielle, Shams and I on board. She, a quiet nineteen-year-old from Quebec City and we, two twenty-nine-year olds from the West Coast Salish.

"You WILL work for passage," declared Captain Charlie in a confident, italicized, Kentucky twang.

His flash of grey eyes like glowing coals, all six foot four and two hundred muscular pounds of him. At fifty, he still had a head full of brown hair, was deeply tanned pink and towering, and Sirius never left his side, teeth exposed at all times.

"I've only let you onto my boat because I think I can get along with you. If not, I WILL whip your ass."

We left early morning at seven and I had the first shift. Steered the forty feet of fiberglass, wood and metal out the harbour without so much as a prayer into Caribbean wind—the audacity. We launched in such a quickness that even our families had no clue of our crossing. Mujeres to Miami by way of the Gulf of Mexico. Weather predictions showed easy twelve-knot winds from the southeast.

But Gulf Stream swift. She run both way. Fastest ocean current on Earth bringing fire from south to north with power greater than all the world's rivers. And as soon as we reached open waters, the wind gathered strength. Within half an hour we were at thirty-, forty-, fifty-knot gale winds! Furious waves hit the boat from twenty feet above. Fear and seasickness set in strong as we took turns—one steering and another keeping watch in three-hour shifts.

Back on Isla Mujeres, Shams and I had spent weeks in the open-air marina bar getting drunk on Dos Equis with sailors, or sometimes quietly bored with each other under the thatch-roof waiting for a job opening, a black cat for company and tree frogs the only high-pitched sounds. Late one night, a gang of kinky French couples in their retirement years—the kind willing to go gladly on their way assuming a gentle fifteen-knot wind from the southeast—invited us onto their boat for wine and sausages. Loud, mocking laughter came from deep within their bottles.

I kept saying, "We can work for passage to the U.S. or Europe or—"

"*Tu n'as aucune idée, ma belle. Il n'y a pas deux vagues qui se ressemblent,*" said one of the drunken Frenchmen. You have no idea, my dear. No two waves are alike.

All around us now, rain and titan blue swells struck the boat with high white caps and squall lines keeping us at permanent forty-five-degree angle with death. We ran the engine hard against the rain to keep death at bay.

Sometime before sunrise that first night, I caught sight of a freighter on the horizon. Hailed them on the radio to announce our presence. They did not answer. I vomited. Hailed again. Nothing. Were they not looking? They seemed almost on a collision course and the storm had made us all but invisible on busy Yucatán shipping lanes.

Ten minutes had passed by the time the freighter hailed back and promised to give us wide girth to starboard, but I had already adrenalined and expelled even that which I did not have.

The wind roared and the boat soared on its diagonal side all next day and night again. The motion lifted toxins out of me like clockwork as I steered. The brightest pockets of star constellations in the night sky made no difference. I was exhilarated and ill among the swells, high rollers and increasing wind speed in the middle of Absolute. Don't take your eyes off the compass or depth gauge even in three a.m. night!

What is freedom on my feet doing? Living a life for joy and abandon worse than any I could ever encounter or survive. Whether you paint your body or your palm, there is some human water lost somewhere. Freedom, my friend, is on this page. Take one step toward it and it runs toward You.

Visible and invisible, these journeys are meant for the perpetual moment to be met without hesitation, only with passion and verve. Ha! Let us see what the nauseous night brings.

Just then, dolphins jumped into a sacred air stampede at the bow of the boat in pearl moonlight. Two, three, a dozen angels in flight. Proper wild luminosity. Astonishment. The clear light when matter is both at its peak and disappears, a precursor to tears, the inner ocean escaped.

It was early afternoon when I rose next day from the bunk that I shared with Shams. Below deck, every crevice, cabinet, hook, shelf and pumpable toilet served essential functions, but none of it assured me.

I climbed up the narrow steps to find Captain Charlie at the helm and Sirius at his side. Without a word, he pointed at something behind me, and I turned to see the silver underbellies of tiny birds above—actually, flying fish in self-propelled leaps from port to starboard, blue to blue, mahi-mahi to frigate. Their wing-like fins at once extended and completely still in the middle of air.

Alongside the boat, shiny striped skipjack tuna moved in unified schools one fathom down. Up ahead, gelatinous Portuguese man o' wars dove at our constant arrival. Later, when we neared Cuba, hundreds of tiny phosphorescent moon jellies floated up to the surface. Captain Charlie grabbed the binoculars and spotted a small boat stationed beside a freighter in the distance and, "Make sure they don't see us, or they'll kill us all," he warned.

Waves crashed into the cockpit as I steered in the dark again another night, another storm, all of it one liquid hallucination. Muscles pushed to exhaustion, upper arms screaming from steering with the windvane against high gusts, thighs and knees on fire from holding onto anything solid as the boat sliced through international waters on a perpetual slant. Somewhere in the constant sickness, the confusion of waves, pots and pans screaming below deck, I gave up.

No land in sight, no sight in dark. Empty, staring at the compass when we had barely reached the middle of the Gulf. This is when the meek in me says: this is too much, I'm doing this, but really, I cannot. O Ancestors, where are your ceremonies? Please, I need them now.

Captain Charlie offered, "This is when you learn that there's nothing you can do. It is what it is. It is what it is."

When the waves are one-eyed giants and the boat is at angle for days and you have no rest from hanging on for dear life and heaving every hour on the hour, soaking wet, purge it all—even that which you do not have.

Time is of no consequence. Freedom the only goal. This is a reminder of the Middle Passage and our unique relationship to water and drowning. Keep your face to the wind and your eyes on the horizon. Look for dolphins to give good morning and good night. Mourn the human beings that were thrown overboard, Ancestors. If necessary, gather yourself into the sea so as to have no more fear of it.

Shams relieved me from duty at six in the morning. He was distant and calm, my opposite. I tried to sleep. There was none.

After seventy-two hours we reached the Dry Tortugas. Shams made me a processed cheese sandwich, and I devoured it. The only thing I had digested since leaving dry land three days before. We dropped anchor per instructions and stayed the night. A thin veil of salt had coated us completely. The chrome of the boat was jeweled with it. Mineral stars. Our skin itched with quartz.

"O the beauty of the world," sighed Shams, and all the day was crystalline.

That night, we bathed in the clear place where the Gulf of Mexico meets North Atlantic. Took a cockpit shower together in the waxing moonlight of the deserted Middle Key. Shams caught my breath in the saline wind. We had come from highest squalls and without warning, everything had turned calm, as if something between us had died.

Next morning, I could just make out the first red rays of daylight on the eastern horizon. We took our time motoring past Marquesas Keys and the weather cleared completely by the time we docked at Key West to replenish supplies.

"I don't date women my own age because at fifty, they've all let themselves go," said Captain Charlie between cockpit pushups. I counted two hundred.

Later, the captain's baritone came from inside the belly of the boat, "Who wants to play a game of chess? I'm gonna open up a can o' whoop ass."

After anchoring overnight at Boot Key, the seventh day was easy. We hoisted sails and the huge, freestanding genoa, caught a meditative wind, and I lay on bagged sails letting the sun do its business on my brown skin. That night we ate fresh mackerel on deck under a shameless vermillion sunset coming into Rodriguez Key.

On the tenth day we arrived at Miami under full moon, a city which made no sense at all. Its pastels and plastics and neon skyline pushed us quickly out. I tossed full packets of birth control pills and Accutane in the motel bin and we jumped into air.

I can't remember how we chose Paris. Perhaps Shams had chosen it and I had simply chosen him. In the end, it was nothing but a suspension of disbelief. An Atlantic's upward curve. That blue hip viewed from the sky—strewn and unrestrained. A new silence between us now, a continent before us. Spring rains came down hard as we landed at Charles de Gaulle.

Shams and I moved quickly toward our own Babel, the tower leaning into our arrival. The end always near. The change of heart cannot be disguised.

# Three

*Et le printemps m'a apporté l'affreux rire de l'idiot.*
And spring brought with it the dreadful laugh of the idiot.

–Arthur Rimbaud
UNE SAISON EN ENFER, A SEASON IN HELL

# The Flood

ALONE IN THE LATIN QUARTER, a wallflower pressed up against grey cut stone, an elite backpack about the feet, flamboyant people dashed around me like human caffeine in the street. Standing downwind from l'Hotel de Médicis, I was catatonic. Face in a slow distortion sadness, nausea rising up throat, a hot bubble just behind the eyes. I left Shams, or did he leave me?

The sun blinded. Stabbed me right through the clouds on that April spring morning. I tried to shoulder my baggage as all grace. Refuge anyone? Nothing remained solid. The body a bag of lava, weak, unable to carry the load, helpless and incapable of asking for help—what rot.

I waited wallside until all the pigeons had left the area. Peeled myself from the stones and dragged my body around devouring streets de l'Épée, l'Assas, Passage d'Enfer, rue Monge. Paris catacombs to the left and cat-walkers to the right. Up ahead, at the tip of Jardin des Grands Explorateurs, I found a hidden bench under cherry blossoms for my dumbfoundedness. Legs shut down. Head bowed but without intent, only shame. I sat for hours without moving, without meditation. Guts gathered mid-chest, a yellow fist, heavy as a punched sun.

By early evening, I had raised myself up and found a way into a medieval palace among palaces built out of rock for the wealthy. The kind of high-end, neglected mansion where you scaled a steep, crackling, wooden staircase and fell apart in a low-ceilinged attic room, barely giving thanks for the money in your pocket.

The walls, carpet and sheets rose pink, the view in ruins. Les Arènes de Lutèce, first-century remains of a Roman amphitheatre, no less. Even there, guards committed slaves, women and poor folks to the higher tiers. Little did they know we get the best views from up here. The writer can only ask for a desk facing open sky and a torrent of shame at the ready. African ancestors at the listening. Notebook open and pencil like a starting pistol. Wine. Music of Mind. Hell all else.

My prayer thrusts aside those who have no hope beyond small deaths, and so I let myself be seized by fruition and fruitlessness. I let myself cry out with open mouth and closed eyes as I expel myself from paradise.

Labour was tough, separation slow. It's the damn placenta I couldn't shake! It leadened me like an extra organ that should have been temporary. Pulled at my eyelids at inopportune moments. No amount of water or wine could ever wash away all this blood.

All the oceans drain away now. Tears are torrents from stone. Amniotic fluid for no one. My percentage lessens. Whites become fire, fire becomes blood, blood becomes placenta cast out from below. I swell in one place, and in another, I am barren.

No strength. Weak with meat and sadness. A black beast, orifices swollen at all times from eye to clitoris. I am at the silent door of exile, how to take the first step?

# Cooked

In the name of Paris in the springtime
In the name of the tears shed by the prophets of God


What do I do now that I've left my lover for a room
with a view? I'm alone in this Paris hotel, drunk and
waiting. Dervish, where is your arc of return? Where
is the source of my flavour? The source of that which
enriches. I remember the day when you first appeared to
me in the tavern. All smooth and working a mean conga.
Slim and dangerous. A grazing of your fingers on my
right arm and the cooking began. You scooped me up
in rituals I hadn't known before. Fed me meals of such
divinity—and I'm known for my gluttony. The divorce
made me ugly. It increased my waist size. Created arms
that did nothing above my head, served only to lift bread
and chocolate and liquor to lips. Bread and chocolate
and liquor to lips. I tried hard not to be at the mercy of
fragments, food or yesterday's mental actions but

In the name of Paris in the springtime
In the name of the tears shed by the prophets of God


What do I do now that I am a solitary traveller, and a poor one at that, hiding under a crust of cautionary sense? A woman in the possible violence of night in new countries. Even old churches here sport gargoyles projected from above to watch over you. But I've got no one to watch my back but my own tattoo. I'm a pilgrim in new landscapes. Travel is a good ritual, like prayer. They are both examples designed to calm the body, focus the heart. Rituals are reminders. Our movement from gross to subtle. *Inshallah*, we find the most beautiful ones but


In the name of Paris in the springtime
In the name of the tears shed by the prophets of God


What do I do now? I will carry myself up from the ocean floor 'cause I got me energy since you closed the door! I will leave the city at full moon. Leave the mistrals, the columns of dog droppings on winding streets, gargoyles at every head thrown back. Gargoyles ain't all that! They are lost lovers jutting from memory with jaws open, ready to get fat. Keep the memory solid. Use as a tool to remove garbage from the Straight Path. Let the gargoyles keep their watch in all their uniqueness and wrath. This magic is real. It comes from my heart, it fills out my hands. It stirs the spoon in the pot, the pencil on the page. It prevents the rot, burns the lead away. This burning is real. There is no end to it, and this burning eventually becomes sweet but

In the name of Paris in the springtime
In the name of the tears shed by the prophets of God

I go round and round in this pot you threw me in, and I thought I could swim. Now you're no longer the chef and I look up to see who's stirring and it's the hand of God working the spoon of me. I see now, this is the meal of me that I offer as alms. The more I get cooked, the tastier I become. And so I let myself be seized. None of this can be undone. I submit myself to True Love, so that the meal of me can belong to everyone.

# Seclusion

AFTER THREE DAYS I climb down from the attic and straight into the middle of a protest against the rise of the far right. Swept up inside one million people occupying boulevard St. Michel with fists punched upward, placards and cries sounding out "No to fascism! No to fascism!" Beating drums a blend of European and North African rhythms. A call for the reordering of order. The cry eternal since cities. Thousands of riot police at the ready. We have seen this before.

The scope of human breath alone fills me with fear. From inside the masses I aim my gaze above the crowd. Look! Chimerical birds perched on their moons. They know I am still alive. Cursed hybrids, upscale monsters sitting coy on Notre Dame's façade. They offer only a gallery of hell above an arc of flying buttresses.

I don't want anyone's looking. I want solitude, intoxication, love from those who reject me and love for those who deserve me. There is an order which surpasses. What is it?

Wasn't there a young man beside me a second ago who made my sex resound? Now hirsute in full view. I am witness to my first silver pubic hair. He missed out. Too bad I had cast him out of l'Hotel de Médicis, or did he cast me?

Everything that occurs becomes poetry, whether by crime or accident. Even my hatred is transformed. The laws of love may elude, but I will get through this theatre, this flower of folly.

# This Work of Destruction

I LEAVE ONE LEFT BANK for another. Avignon is surrounded by thick, stern walls and massive towers. No one will find me here. I am papal deep inside the beige commune, protected even from a flooding Rhône. Inside the medieval ramparts, high on Rocher des Doms, safe behind bars.

Within city walls, I am free to move around clandestine among craft market stalls at Place de l'Horloge. I turn down a slim, stone lane peppered with mopeds, and emerge at the house of popes. White pigeons pursue black pigeons in the courtyard of honour and all miss my head by an inch. I look left, right. Still no sign of Shams. Seven days have passed.

Le Palais des Papes is bellicose, corpulent, a monument to awe and fear. Halls of gothic proportion. Architectures of genocide. Opulence at all expense. Torture, worship and luxury all spoken in the same barbaric breath. My lineage of ghosts tugging at both coattails, working hard to make me remember the ones who lost the war, the ones written out of the story, the ones taken away. The many sides to one story.

The children of German tourists run ahead of me, then behind me, and then ahead again through endless galleries. They point at me, giggling. My brown body, black locks moving and not moving among the spirits. Gliding less than visible through twenty-five dining halls, changing rooms, dungeons and chapels of bloody history that have both enslaved me and are my family. Rooms are repeated. I look right, left. Still no sign of Shams.

Only pale children with axes peering down at me from proud paintings. Short-legged revolutionaries with misshapen noses holding steadfast onto swords. I escape to the medicinal gardens when suddenly, a naked, muscular, porcelain Jesus appears above with arms outstretched in statuesque suffering. We are all in want of touch and service.

I look up. Still no sign. I look back. The fortress, a work of destruction. Empty, too big for itself, out of use and useless if not shared. But it accepts my celibacy and melancholy with open arms today, even as I am nailed to my own ego. The remedy is death. But how to complete the task?

Find a new skin for the old ceremony. *La Alla LaLa* said the voice from the other side of the story. Any cloaked poet would approve.

# Eurafrican

STUDYING THE CHARTS again to assess my position on Earth, it was now May and I moved quick from commune to coast. When you don't know where to go and the motherland is right beside you, there is no choice. Only African descent asking to be the future. The pilgrimage, the risk of no-risk, an arc of diasporic return.

As soon as I stepped aboard *The Marrakesh*, I went missing between Sète and Tangiers in torn skin. The ferry moved without moving. Disappearing coastline was the only indication of in-betweenness. In the constant wind, my senses caught fire and seeped through the skin.

The ship's engines roared and we heaved into Mediterranean past trawlers from Istanbul, Cape Town, Port-aux-Français and Singapore. Passengers on deck waved as wind poured through the cloth openings. Muslim robes took flight. I exchanged one continent for another, again.

Rock of Gibraltar to starboard, Moroccan Rif Mountains to port, an African daughter returning home with faded complexion, a failure at love but free, despite a clutching ego and wandering coins in the pocket.

I gave France a parting prayer but the French passengers interrupted with volume alone. A high-timbred attitude attained only with a sound passed down through generations. Everyone sounds louder when you are silent. I am a stranger to both tourists of conspicuous consumption and family tables of ten. So many robed women and men around me seem content, the waiter even more so. Ya Mustafa! Remind me this peace.

Solitude escapes me with every bat of the eyelash, every turn of the head. I tried for it in the corner of the small, four-person cabin but people followed me even there. We swayed on internal seas for two days, our windowless room smelled of feet and women whispering. But when the others left, their rose scent subsided and my own foul musk remained.

I resorted to self-mutilation and self-worship all at once. Checked my mutating countenance in a discreet compact, attracting no attention but that of God. I applied bronze dust with annoyance and vanity over my shifting blemishes. Should I have abandoned the medicine for my skin in Miami? Are these sores acceptable? Light comes into play again. How does it affect the cheek, the forehead? Are my acne scars visible roots? Are the protrusions visible in these shadows? I have all the side effects and still the original condition. Everything dry, cracked, blood at the edge, philtrum red, womb ruined. Side effects forever. Who will offer remedy for my pains? My vain condition is turning me into a prisoner, and what to do in a prison but write.

# Burst

THE CALL TO PRAYER came early this morning. Two German tourists ate shakshuka and drank Stork beer in their stupor after having been awakened by it at five a.m. Loudspeakers amplified the *azan* from the mosque off Plaza Uta El-Hamman. *Fajr* is not for infidels or unbelievers, but I cannot be certain, I am still sleeping.

This Rif mountain shields itself in cloud and homes are painted lunar blue. Chefchaouen is a heaven for tourism and inner worlds alike. The language barrier is a rich, obstacled Riffian Berber. I took a room in the medina.

"The time for women in the hammam is now," said the living image of my Antiguan grandfather, shoveling perfumed cedar into the oven as I walked past.

There was a cold which touched bone that morning. The bow of defeat, the curved tree, the hanging mirror

51

on a whitewashed wall, slippery cobblestones lend themselves well to a fallen glance from an indigo man in a snow white djellaba.

"This is the land of God!" said Mustafa, refilling my teacup from most high. If I were well, I would invite him to sit with me and sip mint tea under this shy, textiled overhang. There is enough space in this cloud for all, I see it.

In a burst I find all music, all senses, all humours, as all blood, phlegm, choler and melancholy escape unwarranted. Be silent now, I say to myself. Observe and allow yourself to be observed. Leave the common skin to itself. Be modest. Look, don't touch. Listen.

O women! Limit not your movements. Lift your robes and run into the mountains! Shriek in response to Barbary apes and ALLAH! We are here! We are gold! Give us only a little Truth serum and we shall release ourselves unto you, O Great Spirit of Creativity.

May these troubles invite you into life as a poetic event with each tiny movement fundamental to the next. We move from sea to sun to inner space. There is a secret knowledge inside the body framework. The corporeal disappears. The secret remains. Throw this scent of joy and death to all on the Path.

Floating on the gathered pebbles now, Shams is whirling above and Atlantic gallops below, I am undulating on the pavement, or perhaps Mustafa's put something in the tea.

## Shams, the Bird

FORTY DAYS PASSED and still no sign of Shams. I laid down the blue shawl and pulled on the black. Both of us twenty-eight when we met at the tavern and, by thirty, Shams had left me there alone to discover the real meaning of intoxication. My own alcoholism was only a precursor.

None of my friends liked him. I couldn't understand why, nor did I care. I was in a parallel universe. Fallen inside one person outside of time for years. The kind of love story that cannot last with one person, but can last without one. Impact itself comes later to all who survive the initial blow.

Shams stroked my bare shoulder with his edge of hand one night at Bukowski's Bar on the Drive in Vancouver and I never again wanted anything more. We sometimes made love six times a day. There was poetry in all of our actions. My face was clean, body strong, a perfume of youth and immortality about the place. Nothing in this world but him. Nothing in the next.

"Don't you want to be worshipped?" Shams had asked one rainy afternoon after making love. I could not answer. Only he could render me both eloquent and speechless.

"I'm going to visit some friends tomorrow. Do you want to come?"

With Shams, everything was yes. His breath, wisteria before the hummingbird has come to it. Musk, a touch of rose and pine after the rains. Honeyed mint and rich, a maple syrup salmon on the fingertips pressed to nose after acts of love. His body needed my touch, his head, my hand on the temples, his smell, my sense of it.

It was a modest, church-like building on a Friday afternoon in spring 2001. The Quaker Meeting House lay unassuming under grey skies, giant cedar branches reaching up into a sprinkle of rain. Coast Salish is its own kind of cool and moist. We ducked into the back basement door, and everything went quiet. Passed through a large, old-fashioned dining room and kitchen.

Like a glutton, I ate everything, but Shams received the taste. I ate the thunderclap of him. The storm I missed the night before in my sleep, the madness of it. The surrender. The essential oil. Call it what you will, without belief, without faith, call it only with absurdity! Call it love on all levels of cells, gustatory or otherwise. This is the way I want to live. This ceaseless prayer. A constant surprise. The way Shams would arrive unannounced at the office ready to make love on the desk once everyone had gone home. The surprise party, saffron walls, a new world of music, the love poems, the poetry of the Sufis. The music that unlocked in me. All of our golden sections at once. The gaze and the freedom like a clever rubbing of hands.

I followed Shams up the narrow, vintage flight of stairs. The landing opened onto a spacious hall where dozens of people sat on carpets and sheepskins on the smooth wooden floor. At the far end, two long-haired, mustached men were speaking in a tongue I did not recognize. Shams and I approached, I held onto him tight. He put his hand to his heart and bowed slightly before the men; they did the same. One of them glanced at me with Lightning. And then we sat down beneath the giant bay windows. When the elder spoke, his companion would translate from Turkish to English. He asked if anyone in the room had a dream to tell. I disappeared.

Without a word, Shams had brought me to a gathering of Sufis. I never left that room. I am in that room and that room is in me. It is the tavern that was sought all along. Home, but not just yet.

Perhaps this was not magic. Even Shams, the magician had quit the area and only the tools were left behind: drums, a reed flute, sheepskin, songbooks. I, the result of moving weapons, rhythmic with white powder, muscle, focus and the unpreventable. What creation is within us! What tones! Astronomical perfections were achieved with Shams: prediction, remembrance, flight, alchemy, Absolute Music of Life. *Proportiones Musicae*. I can't remember why my eyes followed you, or how I knew you were well. I can't remember why my eyes followed you, or how I knew you were well.

# The Mohammedan

CROSSING THE RAS EL MAA, Amazigh women washed clothes by the shore and eyed me with due suspicion. I climbed into the mountain overlooking the powdered blue cubes of Chefchaouen.

The footpath was strewn with pale pink rosebay, poppies and occasional mint, at times the high grasses swallowed us up along the slim, earthen upward arc like a pebbled wave. One by one, men sitting sedentary by the path or descending the mountain took sexual aim. I moved past, trying not to invite or excite. Climbed hurriedly up the Rif.

Placing a foot inside a derelict Spanish mosque, the twelfth century ruined walls were peppered with cobalt graffiti. Roofless, the sky was in full view. Sun giving everything away. There was a spot among the rocks and as I settled in to let the star do its business, a man walked out of cloud a stone's throw away from me.

He was sunken-cheeked and slim. Trim, black beard and skin the colour of Medjool dates. A white cotton shirt, dark emerald vest and small leather bag across the chest, his black turban had the end hanging down between the shoulder blades.

He stood immobile with his back to me, catching his breath after the rugged walk uphill. Turning, he startled and approached, gently. I held out an open bag of fresh figs.

"*As-salamu alaykum*," he greeted, putting his hand to his heart before plucking a fig from the bag.

"*Wa alaykumu s-salam*," I replied.

Mohammed was a weaver from a family of weavers who spoke Spanish, Arabic and a dialect of Riffian Berber. We sat together outside the ruined mosque and conversation had barely begun when he removed a long, tan, leather pouch from his bag. Two wooden pipes and a red clay bowl fit tightly together to make one long sebsi. He dipped the bowl into a tiny sack of sticky hashish, lit the end away from wind, sucked quick and heavy, then passed the sebsi to me. Strong and sweet, rich and fragrant with mint. Afternoon deepened and my lips cracked bloody in the stark rays. We ate figs that melted in the mouth like warm strawberry jam and sat sprawled in the cradling sun.

"I was born in the year of the elephant," he recounted. "My father died before I was born. When I was still a baby, I was sent to live in the desert with a Bedouin family. When I was still very young, my mother also died. Then, my grandfather and uncle took me in and raised me. We were very poor. I did not starve, but in the end, I traveled, went looking for knowledge in far-away places."

Mohammed removed a small reed flute from his shirt pocket and began to play. Quarter tones in actual air. Time elastic and the call to prayer arrived late that day, it was already past four. Mohammed excused himself, stood up from the rock, walked a short distance and paused. He turned left and right. Set his vest on the ground, and began the *salat* prayer.

A young boy joined him. When Mohammed bowed, the young boy bowed, and when he stood up straight, so did the boy. They both prostrated, and I too, prostrated inside myself.

The day glistened. Mohammed plucked his vest from the grass and returned to sit beside me. The boy disappeared. We continued talking as before, but now each breath was a new worship. Today was the day for prayer, not for the future, nor the past, but for the All Invisible Present.

We hiked down the mountain into town through the cemetery. Calm, azure headstones were arranged perpendicular to Mecca. The wind increased around us and my indigo shawl exploded wing-like in the lush green Rif. Children played soccer alongside the graves.

We arrived at a domed door in the blue medina. Mohammed's home was crowded and cavernous both. One cube of natural light shone through the front door window to illuminate the vast, single room. On the far wall, two couches and a low table; to the left, a tiny kitchen counter and hotplate. There was no washroom or running water. The far wall was piled high with textiles of all sizes and colours. At the centre of everything, a large, wooden, four-poster, hand-operated loom that reached the ceiling.

We smoked kif in the illuminated black. Suddenly, Mohammed jumped up swift and eager. Entering the loom from beneath, he climbed into the walled-in bench and began to explain its inner workings, the intertwined harps of Yemeni cotton, the beauty of Omani thread, linen and green floss silk.

Settling in at the helm, Mohammed plucked the neatly folded apron before him, tied it ritually around his waist, closed his eyes and took a deep breath. All at once, his whole muscular body activated the loom with the ease of a concert pianist. A ceremony of speed, agility, push and pull instrumental, the loom beating out a slow rhythmic pattern. Practical magic, austere and religious. He transformed the cotton into a pattern of red and black stripes, like all traditional Yemeni cloths. Mohammed became an active metaphor, hitting keys just right, Earth itself in rotation on its axis. I became hypnotized. The *azan* sounded, "*Allaaaaaaahu Akbar!*"

It was time. Mohammed reached for a striped silver and blue textile. As he covered me with the cloak, he whispered, "It is a fountain of magic and power."

We walked side by side for a moment into the night until *as-salamu alaykum* Mohammed disappeared. I never saw him again.

# Hassan's Tower

RIDING AN EARLY MORNING bus to Rabat, something happened to my face en route. Although I struggled not to speak or draw attention to myself, oil seeped out of me unannounced. In the North African heat, I developed a strange rash—bright red pustules sliced themselves across both cheeks down to the chin, like burns.

In the mirror, the sight of my own face frightened me. I considered staying indoors out of embarrassment. The face of God, ashamed of itself.

At the time of my affair with Shams, I had smooth, simple skin, the product of pharmaceuticals. The day of our separation, my condition returned. *Une chance que je l'ai quitté à temps. Mais dommage que cette peau de lait noire ne soit pas éternelle.* Good thing I left him on time. But how unfortunate that this black milk skin is not timeless.

I picked at the rash out of habit and sacrifice, then applied makeup to the tiny wounds. Held my head up just high enough and walked the city streets of white, sanitized Rabat looking for a woman-friendly restaurant. Men continued to accost, seeking company, seeking refuge. It took only one to intrude just right.

*"Bonsoir,* can I walk with you?"

My head turned left and a tall man had materialized beside me. A master of youth, loose in blue jeans and a white, embroidered tunic, black hair gelled in place and a beard trimmed fresh, though I detected a disarming musk about him that was not from cologne. A player ready for all kinds of play.

*"Non, merci."* No, thank you. I increased my pace and he did the same.

*"N'ayez pas peur. Moi c'est Hassan. Et vous? Vous êtes marocaine?"* I mean you no harm. I'm Hassan, and you? Are you Moroccan? "Where are you from? Wait, let me guess, Spain? u.s.? Is it your first time in Rabat? While you are here you must visit Hassan Tower. It's dedicated to my ancest—"

"You look like you're dressed to go out on a date, my friend," I blurted, interrupting him. "Don't keep anyone waiting."

*"Elle parle, Alhamdulillah! On prend un thé ensemble?"* She speaks, Thank God! Can I invite you for tea? "Well, actually, I was going to meet some friends at a café, it's a mixed place, you would like it. Would you join me? My friends are very sweet except when they pull the rug from under you…" his voice trailed off and I took the opportunity to cross the street. He followed, still. "So tell me, what do you do?"

"I'm trying to be a writer," I said, slightly defeated, slowing down now.

*"Aha! Si j'avais une feuille de papier vierge, je voudrais que vous y écriviez tout ce que vous désirez."* If I had a blank sheet of paper, I would want you to write whatever you desired on it. He paused, grinning. "Are you married? I've been known to unmake marriages."

"Please, I want to walk alone now."

*"Mais vous êtes clairement intéressé, et moi aussi. Je crois que vous êtes charmante, mais pas belle; athlétique, mais*

*gourmande.*" But you are clearly interested, and so am I. I believe you are charming, but not beautiful; athletic, but a glutton.

I covered my head and ran quickly into night. Could hear his voice calling out from behind me as I crossed the street, "*Inshallah,* someone back home is looking out for your best interest, better than you yourself!"

I ran to my old friends Solitude and Vanity no less, part conditioning, part condition. The *azan* sounded, nothing more—everything shifted, abated. Was I destined to get drunk in my room again? I didn't come to the motherland for solitude.

I must find some magic to repair this condition, this unease. What do I do aside from beg Shams in dark rooms on cold nights? Who am I even speaking to? I have no personal description. The tears keep breaking past the barrier, nothing human can contain them. I've forgotten how to pray, I am praying. Shams appears. Disappears.

This work of living is bitter fruit. Cavernous empty. Try not to think, not to think, not to think. I'm only falling apart slightly now. It comes and goes little by little, you see, mostly in private. I'm not even present in this room. Just here to disappear. One day, a good feeling will again overwhelm, *Inshallah*.

That night in the dream, Shams is wearing a yellow shirt. He enters and begins shouting at me, gesticulating, saying that my story is false and that he's heard enough. I approach him and begin twisting his arm to make him believe. As I do this, I wake up.

Next day the mirror showed no signs of the rash—it's as if I had imagined it. The meaning of the message is lost, but the picture of it remains.

# False Grave

MARRAKESH IS MYTH made tourist. The high-ringing tones of darbouka soared into air above as I walked undercover in the rhythmic medina camouflaged in the usual scars. The square of Jemaa el-Fnaa in afternoon Anti-Atlas sun is a lion always hungry. Public snakes entranced by sweet wind. Water-sellers in regalia free for photos. Hardcore acrobat troupes in human pyramids among robed elders and colonial imposters without fail or organization, but perfection nonetheless. I include myself. Which self? The African daughter or the ambiguous tourist? And just then sounds divine and scents overwhelming of burnt pigeon feathers, clay, cumin, chili, rose and white smoke intoxicated me. I would leave it all behind for what I had lost.

I moved through Bahia Palace and the surrounding shops of sharp pyramid displays in cinnamon, turmeric and paprika. Fragrant dust piled conical high in defiance of gravity. Dry pepper and purple eggplant skin garlands hanging over cubes of musk, stained glass bottles of forest green and royal blue. I stopped in awe and the shopkeeper who greeted me knew nothing of spice or herbal medicine, but something of art.

"If you have time, I would be very glad to host you at my studio. It's nearby," he put forth, appearing to float inside his long white djellaba.

Within minutes, I was following another man named Hassan down tall, narrow alleys of good, thick mud into the Mellah, the Jewish quarter. A walled city inside the city.

He flowed as I followed awkwardly. He was in his forties, but appeared older due to a slight limp and some extra weight around the middle. No matter, his grace was compounded by lemon yellow babouches peeking out from underneath his long robe.

We passed through the door of his studio and into a cool, dimly lit room. Uneven white walls domed a small sitting area. Pastel canvases, painted plates and Amazigh jewels covered every available surface. In the paintings were animals, human forms. The haram hidden inside abstracts.

Hassan had studied visual arts and German literature in Berlin. He worked in the spice shop by day and painted by night with the support of friends and family.

"Colour and shape are everything to me! This is my service. This is why I am alive."

And with the propane stove and kettle at the ready, Hassan began the tea service as we settled in across from each other on pillows. Full cups, he lit the sebsi to open our afternoon.

"When I was born, my grandfather sacrificed a ram and gave it to the poor in the village. My mother shaved my head and gave the weight of my baby hair in silver as alms. Can you believe it?" he said, beginning to laugh, "I am bald now, but as a baby I had too much hair!" We both laughed.

I inhaled more kif than I should have and my silence turned loud. I may have revealed too much. My heart lay bloody and broken, gross on short sleeves in the face of Hassan's calm, internal landscape.

"I speak to Shams through my own voice at night!" I cried. "Can he hear me? What is happening? What is this? My chest hurts. I know that eventually I will have to stop speaking to him as if he were in the room, right? Why did he leave me? Where did he go?"

Hassan waited a long time before responding. I wept in the cool quiet room.

"You are going through something very beautiful. Once you surrender, you will be like a newborn. It's good that you came to Morocco.

"You know, you would have liked my grandfather. He was an exceptional human being. He and my mother Fatima were very close. You remind me of her. When he died, he was mourned by many. But my mother was left alone in her grief for too long and it drew her so close to death that a few months later, death took her as well.

"On the day, she bathed, put on new clothes, lay down and passed—no ceremony, no prayers, no burial. At her request, there are several false graves to ensure that her true grave is never discovered. You have heard this story before but—"

There came a knock at the door and Hassan got up to answer. The story wasn't finished! Indiscernible voices. An elderly couple entered the room holding a box of almond and rosewater pastries. Khadija, Mohammed, Hassan and I ate sweets and smoked bitter apple tobacco on charcoal, glowing. The rising steam bubbled as we inhaled soft, phenomenal and easy. Peace was no longer fleeting but held us firmly as we blushed near the fire. For a long time, no one spoke. After our meditation, Hassan rose and left the room. He never did finish the story.

Before leaving, the elder Mohammed looked at me and said, "We don't know each other, you and I, but don't worry, you will be all right. Stop crying. Go sit under a cedar and let old woman windchill dry your tears and cool down the interior of your fire. Clouds cover sun, but only for a moment in this garden prone to drought in the desert. Go back to work now. The world of fragrant orange, fig and olive blossom needs your service in order to bear fruit."

# Alive but Emptied of Self

THE CANARY CURRENT SWAYED wide and slow on its way south in the Atlantic distance. The African coastline of the diasporic imaginary all the way down to Senegal before heading back to the outer realms. Looking down over the ramparts, a party of four tourists walked along the beach past the stationary dromedaries in windy Essaouira. They looked tired and hungry but well. Well-fed and dressed with fattened wallets and skin stretched taut and leathery. Even as the men pulled ahead, the women held steadfast onto them—to let go was divorce. I will not let go.

At dusk, I found a spot on the beach and got my own whipping from the falling sun. Moved onto blackened boulders to get near crashing current. The tide came toward me in white, foamed shadows. White waves with arms overthrown, heads back—ever seen a wave like that? Mouths crying open at the fattened half-moon, flinging themselves onto wet sea stones as night covered us all. That Friday wailed of Shams. If I want to keep you, I must use you. Blacken you better than the night, or rather like red snapper, limed, slightly battered, maize then fire to mouth.

After sundown, I found a small family restaurant beneath the sea wall with low tables that only went up as high as the knee. As I folded myself to eat Legnaoui's *tajine de poisson marinée*, a middle-aged American tourist changed seats to sit near me. He got brazen quick by diving straight into tall tales of windsurfing without even asking my name.

"So, I've been all up and down the coast from Taghazout. A place called Killer Point has THE best waves. One time I had a killer whale right beside me. I tell ya, I screamed like a little girl, my adrenaline shot so high. Hey, do you like fig liqueur?"

I forged a complaint about the food to get him to leave me alone but at that moment, he touched my leg under the table. I froze and disappeared.

Was it a dream or a prediction? I reentered the world a few months earlier, among the streets around Plaza de la Constitución as they congested on a warm February day. Shams and I had descended from the Palenque jungles into a Mexico City whose Congress was blocked with cows and a thousand cowboy hats. Farmers were protesting the costs of NAFTA.

A large, thickly mustached man had sat down at the table where Shams had left me for a moment. The wide sweat stains around his arms and chest darkened his blue shirt. He tipped his cowboy hat in my direction.

"*¡Hola guapa! Sabes que aquí en México estamos acostumbrados a las protestas y marchas políticas. No te preocupes.*" Hello beautiful! You know here in Mexico City we are used to protests and political marches. Don't you worry about it.

"*¿De donde eres? ¿Estás sola? ¿Te puedo ofrecer una bebida?*" Where are you from? Are you alone? Can I buy you a drink?

The protesters shouted in unison, "*¡Zapata vive! ¡La lucha sigue!*" Zapata lives! The fight continues!

The sirens sounded, the man's voice intensified and loudspeakers joined in. Suddenly Shams returned to save me from purchase. He touched my leg under the table. It is the only touch I want.

At that moment in Essaouira, I swallowed the lump in my throat and removed the American man's hand from my thigh. I returned to my meal though it was now bubbling inside my stomach. Without a word,  he had secretly ordered fig liqueur for the both of us, and when it arrived at the table, I was hit all at once with a swell of nausea. I ran away.

Barely up the stairs of l'Hotel Majestic, when a torrent of saffron mud poured violent out of my mouth and all over the floor of the communal bathroom. A full-bodied flood directed outward—an exorcism, a wound excised.

The stranger had activated my flight response. Triggered old trauma. The body was still rejecting events. What had happened with Shams could not be absorbed.

Acute fever and chills overwhelmed me. I swallowed two tablets of activated charcoal and lay down. Shivering, burning, confused with fire and freezing, I tried to sleep under layers of clothing and blankets. After some time, the nausea returned and my cheeks ballooned as I ran to the sink in my room. This time the bile was black. I fell back to bed, unconscious.

# Dream of a Poet

IN THE DREAM, MY FRIEND the poet Zeechilla the Great had been locked in a closet and was pounding on the door to get out. I opened it but he remained inside with his back toward me, his hands tied behind him. Suddenly his head was twisted around to face me. His bearded mouth moved without a sound, dark eyes wide with surprise. Then his head spun back to normal, but his eyes remained fixed on me, unattached to the face. I began to untie the rope around his wrists and thought that, perhaps, all of this was not natural.

Next morning, I received news that Zeechilla had passed away in Vancouver from unknown causes. It turned me immobile. A poet burning. Someone dipped me in fire. I did not melt, but my skin sizzled. Sores began to form at the surface, glorious red-hot sunspots pulling hair from face. The entire process barely took the eye away from evil. What is it in me, that feels so close to death?

# Old Medicine

BREAD FOR BREAKFAST and vomit for dinner, the next three days were light in protein and dark in bile. I checked my waistline in the mirror—it remained thick. I threw my shoulders back for good measure and took smaller, lighter steps. Head just high enough. There was satisfaction in waiting for the purge to end, to being alive and witness to it.

I could feel a cold coming on as I entered the labyrinthine Essaouira spice souk. Sat down to discourse with the mighty Hakim of the inner circle of apothecaries. Hakim was bewitching, in his early twenties with a wise way about him that was still in development. Tall and lithe with seamless skin the colour of hickory, his beige skullcap rested slightly to one side and his whole blue-robed body followed. A man of gentle ways, he would gaze upward when listening in order to provide the most beautiful answer. He did this now, thought for a long moment before giving me any medicine.

*"Prends ces grains de nigelle avec du miel. Ça te guérira. Le prophète lui-même, Rasūl Allāh Muhammad ʿalayhi s-salām, en a parlé."* Take this black seed with honey. It will heal you. The prophet himself, Muhammad, peace be upon him, spoke about it.

I pressed the tiny nigella seeds to my nostrils and inhaled. Black dots of purifying eucalyptus. Next day, my cold had disappeared and the vomiting ended, though the nausea remained.

In my old age, I turn to old medicine. In return, this encourages young merchants to be confident and seek out older women as possible lovers. Young man, this will greatly enrich you, while also preventing your hand from touching my breast or perhaps inviting it there.

*"Ici, c'est la terre de Dieu,"* said Hakim, filling my teacup from most high without yielding a drop to the table. This is the land of God.

# Husayn's Museum

IT WAS HIGH MIDDAY HEAT when I entered the window-less studio in underground Essaouira. At the narrow entrance, round mirrors hung on either side, each framed with metal, stone, blood and bone—it was not a shop at all. The inner room was sweeping. Rough, whitewashed walls covered with lances and morning stars, aged gold coins and leather saddles, goat skins and faded maps of the Euphrates.

A man knelt immobile at the far end of the cool room. An elongated green djellaba, forehead to the ground in prostration. He did not pause. As he bowed, I bowed inside myself. He was entranced.

What rose from prayer and moved toward me was a beautiful, androgynous Black man, head shaved bald and a face of finely sculpted features with a faint goatee around the mouth. An air of fire and vigour about him, he was quick to charm, claiming an attraction to me in very few words. I responded. He invited me to sit for mint tea and baklava. I could not come to food but it was coming to me. My nausea gave thanks.

Ali was a scribe, I could see the open Quran beside a blank manuscript with the beginnings of long, syrupy handwritten strokes of Arabic calligraphy on the top right.

"All of these artefacts you see here are open secrets," he said, pointing. "Gold leaf Qurans, prayer rugs, arrows... This is what remains from the battle of Karbala." His voice rose and his body straightened.

*"As soon as our souls part from our bodies, you will find out who is most worthy of entering the fire!"* he recited with passion.

I did not understand. I froze inside myself. Ali became calm and poured water gently on a small red-berried plant in the corner.

"Mistletoe. Some parts are poisonous, but the fruits are harmless to birds. Birds gorge themselves and shit the seed wherever their two wings take them. The seeds stick to branches and grow there, taking root wherever they fall. One supports the other. Two wings, *un oiseau*."

A ginger kitten approached and Ali took it in his arms, set it back down near its mother. He poured hot mint tea into our glass cups from high above. The colours in the room changed.

"I was born inside a rock," he said, gazing at some upward vanishing point, "I stayed there with my mother for three days. I don't remember this of course, but it's what they tell me."

He reached for a polished bottle made of camel bone and opened it. The scent of ambergris filled the room with heady perfume.

Unconsciously, I reached for it, but "This is not for sale," said Ali, his voice lush. "Everything here belongs to all of us, freely."

I began to rise and as I did, he stole a kiss. I liked it. Mistletoe. True, his touch was unwarranted, and I was between two worlds on the matter. Though it meant nothing, it was the first intimate touch since the disappearance of Shams.

I was sometimes unsure how to answer these gestures. I thought they were sexual advances but acted as if it were friendship. Always some momentary confusion when faced with a lion of God. Most of the time however, advances were balanced with a gentle kindness and a seductive ability to pour tea. A blend of Islam and virility. Restrained and hedonist both. The finest line. A dot.

Stricken again with old nausea, I moved toward the door, but Ali prevented me from leaving.

*What's yours will find you,* said a voice that was not his. It came from somewhere behind the walls.

"Forgive me," said Ali, stepping aside. Quickly, I ran away.

# Spitting Image

THE CHOIR OF MUEZZINS gave the *al-maghrib* and took the town into painted dusk. A fattened moon hung low above the fish market jetty. Thick, alkali smoke from outdoor grill stands flew up carrying the scent of char and sardines into night. Seagulls screamed with glee at fish guts and tones of Maghrebi Arabic did business by the side of the path.

Walking further down to the tip of the jetty everything turned quiet, the fishing boats swayed and old men looked silently out onto Atlantic.

Returning up the crescent of the port, the Sqala du Port appeared at the place where the peninsula meets land. A bastion that sold slaves descended from Bilal. Sons of Bambara. Gnawa. Different fort but same trade, like all the human traffic stops up and down this West African coastline and up the other side.

Just then a haggard, blue-eyed, blond dreadlocked man shuffled up beside me and began a verbal assault. I asked to be left alone. He threw his venom high, shouting that he despised all foreigners and that I was racist. He spat on me and stomped away.

I did not react. Kept walking, wiping the saliva from my cheek inside my heart, throwing aside the sword, restraining the inner fight. Soon after, a new stranger pulled up alongside and apologized. He alleged that his friend was drunk and not in control of his actions. Kept my eyes dead ahead. Retired to my rented room. Your body does not command me.

That night I tightened my locks in a gesture of protection. Took my time twisting each nappy rope into a Bantu knot. Slept with my head pulled tight. Next day at the unravelling, the locks fell on my shoulders in power ringlets, a separate helix each. DNA reaching out. Tiny whirling dervishes about the head. A coil of snakes sheathed and bulletproof, ready to conjure, turn you into stone. It was my birthday.

I returned to Hakim who had become a confidante overnight and he placed a gris-gris around my neck—

three small leather pouches of yellow sulfur enclosing an inscription from the Quran to ward off evil.

As he hung the charm on me, an elder passed by and bent forward. Waving a tattooed, arthritic finger, she said, "*Ce gris-gris là, il est bon pour la magie noire et la magie blanche. Baraka Allahu feek.*" That gris-gris there is good for black magic and white magic. May God bless you. Then she turned and walked away waving her hand. Her milk apricot breath lingered long after she had gone.

Next evening, I made my way up the ramparts again at sunset and saw men drunk in the streets because wives would not have such behaviour in the home. They hiccupped and threw up gently on the crowded blue fishing boats occupying the port. Navy night descended over the Citadel.

The man who had spat on me approached, skittish, asking forgiveness. I began to walk faster and he sped up to me, promised not to bother me again, then let go.

I knew it was time to leave. A sphere had appeared around me. Where I had been rough, the trade winds had softened, smoothed my skin, relaxed me into myself. Wingspan, the sensation of hovering—even for a moment. Effortless effort. Gliding freedom. Accepting of change, living without expectation, only surprise.

# Lands are Joined at the Handle

"EVERY DAY IS SEPTEMBER 11TH," said the White Rock, British Columbia border guard on that cold January morning when our travels first began. He wouldn't let us cross the U.S.-Canada boundary with our DriveAway car—didn't believe we would actually return it to its owners in Palm Springs. Shams and I had put our lives into storage and taken the road south with only a plan to wander.

We stared wide-eyed at the framed Peace Arch behind him. A hard snow fell to the Coast Salish ground outside as we waited in the clenched, slate grey building to enter the neighbour's yard.

"Your papers are not in order. Who are the car-owners? How long are they staying in the U.S.? What is a DriveAway again?" The guard turned blue in the face to match his uniform.

After three hours, the thing resolved itself and we made it past the longest undefended border in the world. Hugged the I-5 straight into a live Cuban music concert in Seattle that baptismal night, our motel room full of sex.


From one fast-food meal to another, we drove south until Palm Springs opened her desolate gates of golf courses and wind farms in jeweled outlines of sand. A mid-century man-made oasis in the desert. Curious attempts at masking the Absolute. We returned the car to its retired orange-grove owners and pulled out a map. Mexico, Cuba, Mali... I had only wanted to travel the world with my beloved, location was unimportant. Our plans were not our plans at all. His agenda remained hidden, even from himself. First Mexico, then the wind. I should have seen the signs instead of only looking at them.

## Vallée des Roses

BY JUNE, THE GIANT DAMASK rose outside El-Kelaâ M'Gouna was in full late bloom. Thousands of pink Syrian blossoms edged the highway. When we arrived at the end of the line, I was the last person out the van. The High Atlas Mountains were bone dry, air thick with pungent rose from the valley below. Kasbahs ruined and valleys succulent, palm trees rose from rose. I descended ochre rock into the narrow valley of green palm, thorns and heady, blushing petals. A naked boy stopped scrubbing his feet by the riverbanks of Assif n Im'Goun to point me out to his friends. Swimming children stopped their play and laughed. This did nothing to affect me as I floated drunk inside the fragrance of roses that had taken afternoon sun.

Without warning, an older, white-turbaned man in a brown suit jacket appeared from behind the bushes. He lurched at me extending a bouquet of fresh picked roses, slurring his words.

Quickened my step to keep him at bay but he would not leave me alone. I ran. He grabbed at me, missed, grabbed again. Shouting in Arabic, his breath reeked of alcohol. And then a child came down from the time of Muhammad to save me.

The child's name, I later learned, was Jibril, whose beauty alone immobilized the drunken man. Jibril took my hand, kissed it, then pulled me away among the bushes into the valley. The man stood, lurking. He soon disappeared into the pink as Jibril led me home in the clouds through sandstone, stream and edge of valley, every step an upward escape.

Twelve years old and running swift across the land in a long blue skirt and flying fuchsia headscarf. On the other side of the pass, Jibril opened the courtyard gate and we entered a long, apricot-scented garden of tall raspberry hollyhock and oleander. Walked through to the far end and into a long rectangular room with high-beamed ceilings and walls of red mud and crossed straw— African wattle-and-daub architecture of the entire world. Removed our shoes and sat in a corner on carpets and pillows against the cool wall.

Jibril sat beside me, genderless. The sitting room became busy with family. Fertile grandmothers, cherub children with elderly faces—all quiet. We smiled at each other through our shyness.

The only adult male at home that day was Adam. The eldest child of five and Jibril's big brother, he had a strong scent of rose about him. A statuesque, mahogany man with the blushing cheeks of youth, he began the tea service with ease and ritual. Told me how he had been working with his mother in her rose distillery since the age of fourteen. They produced Damask rosewater and essential oil, so he always had that scent about him and so did she, though he barely noticed it now. At twenty, he was still rehearsing his role as head of household while his father was away on business, his mother always with the roses. He prepared the tea and was the only one who spoke with me the entire time, aside from Jibril who told me that I would never have children.

Water boiled in the kettle for the gunpowder green. A tray of clear, cylindrical glasses appeared with a large pewter teapot. A heap of fresh spearmint was pushed inside and then slim shards of sugar were cut by cutlass from a crystalized loaf. Each step precise before the potion was poured from high without a single drop spilled. Perfect froth. Continuous cups. We drank and ate crusty, homemade khubz dipped in nutty argan oil.

By the third cup, the family had dispersed and I was prompted to a smaller room for privacy and Camel Lights. Adam was an attractive man, but I didn't like the way he invited me to lie down on his bed with him. He lay on the mattress while I sat cross-legged on the floor. Told him that I was reading a lot these days and had a copy of Rimbaud's *Poésies* with me.

Looking up at the ceiling he mused, "I like Camus and Verlaine well enough but my favourite book…"

"What is it?"

"*Le Pain Nu* by Mohamed Choukri," he said. "You must read that book while you are here. Choukri left home at eleven to escape an abusive father and was very poor up in the northeast of the country. He was homeless for years on the streets of Tangiers until someone taught him to read and write in Arabic at the age of twenty. It took only one person to change his life. He was the age that I am now."

At that moment, Jibril entered with a tray of wine, water and milk. Adam chose wine and I, milk. Jibril looked at Adam with solace then asked if I would come and play hide and seek. Adam rose from the mattress and invited me to stay the night or return the next day for a hike in the mountains. My skin spoke for me. And with that, he took my hand in his and placed in it a tiny bottle of oil. I bowed.

"Making rose oil is a difficult process that can take a very long time. You have to give up sixty thousand petals in order to produce just one ounce of oil. But it's worth it for the essence of the essence."

The light was fading when Jibril and I made our way onto the path in the valley floor chewing licorice bark inside a crumbling Kasbah left to bake in the sun. The star lowered its head behind the High Atlas Mountains and, up the road, I could just make out the last minivan in the distance. Back at Kelaâ, I could not remember the name of the village where I had just been nor could I find it on any map.

## Mother of Us All

Next day I was the only woman in the streets by six p.m. After a bowl of roasted eggplant tajine, I rose from the warped plastic chair and slipped out the back door of *Restaurant Rendez-vous des Amis*. Seated outside, a robed figure looking out at the desert plateau. Her head turned at my arrival, a Nubian profile.

*"As-salamu alaykum. Bonsoir. Moi c'est Hajar. Je vous en prie."* She motioned to the chair beside her.

Draped elegant in a dark djellaba and Tuareg blue head-scarf, gold loop earrings dripping beside her face, Hajar was a striking woman. The sharpest cheekbones beneath kohl-lined eyes that looked sad yet defiant. Her youth, a regal quality.

"Where are you from, sister?" she asked, smiling.

"Quebec, Canada."

"Ha! I have never met an African from Canada," she confessed. "It must feel good in your heart to be back on African soil, *Mashallah*. Welcome home."

I could not speak.

"I'm a schoolteacher," she continued. "But I miss Egypt terribly, my whole family is there. I came here to work on contract, to get some international work experience, but life is hard for women in Morocco. There is so little education, so little respect. Girls work in the fields and raise enormous families—this is both the beginning and the end. Some girls are completely used up and thrown away. At least the Kelaâ rose harvest is led by women. They grow the rose and distil it. We need more of that and *more than* that—much more."

Hajar taught French, Arabic literature and Quran to children in a nearby village that did not allow any mixing of the unmarried or unrelated sexes. It was an Amazigh village steeped in Sharia law.

"I can't walk down the street beside a male colleague without starting a riot!" she cried.

She had come to Kelaâ to escape both judgment and her Moroccan fiancé with whom she had fallen out of love. She was undertaking an academic examination of marriage and he no longer measured up. Language and communication were her passions and her fiancé was not interested in either.

"I know he loves me deeply. It's just that he was married before and is much older. Sometimes he takes advantage of our difference in age. I can't seem to stand up to him. My own virginity and intellect are not enough. Will never be enough." As if Muslim were fighting Muslim.

"I am traveling to increase my trust in God and my wellbeing, but it is difficult, *Astaghfirullah*. Maybe this is the time for me to make Hajj. But I also just want to be married and be a mother and maybe even a grandmother someday. Don't you?"

The stars had begun to give away their old light. We got up and walked down the main street together while men shot us bewildered looks for our lack of a male chaperone this late in the day. We continued talking about future travels—hers to Mecca and mine to Sahara. Both Absolute.

## Basic Mechanics

BOUMALNE DADES WAS a small town on the edge of desert plateau. The kasbah, once a watchtower for the defensive was now a refuge for strangers. I set down my backpack in the cool room where the walls looked soft and pillowy at first glance but, upon deeper inspection, were solid masses of cracked, coral-red mud and dung flecked with straw.

All the buildings here emerged from the soil, which emerged from the sea. This hotel, an extension of the naked rock. Perched overlooking the oasis, lush green forest stretched serpentine as far as all eyesight. Mars-like rust cliffs protecting us on either side.

After milk coffee for breakfast, I took a collective van deeper into the Dadès Gorges looking for the end of the line. I was the last one out the van again. Ventured out onto the main street without any idea where to begin.

Wandered into a shop where giant translucent quartz and spiralized ammonite fossils commandeered high dusty shelves inside. The shopkeeper offered me a seat and a welcoming tea.

Ahmed had a gentle, shining face, his cheeks full of smile lines. He had been a miner for some years at Imider, the biggest silver mine on the continent. He had little formal education but a wealth of geological and parenting knowledge, having opened this shop when his wife left him with their three young children almost twenty years ago. He had managed with the help of family and friends.

"Where are you going?" he asked.

"I'm running away," I admitted, bowing my head.

"What are you running from?"

"Myself."

"If the mountain won't come to you, then you must go to the mountain. The answers are all around you."

Before I could respond, Ahmed called out to his sons, "Habib! Siddiq! Mustafa!"

Three handsome young men emerged from behind a curtain at the far end, each taller than the next. Habib and Siddiq both in their mid-twenties were followed by the youngest, a towering, six-foot-six Mustafa, who had to bow at the threshold to enter the room.

Ahmed introduced us and asked each one the same question in Tamazight. The elder brothers gave long answers but Mustafa remained silent. Patient. When it came his turn, he bowed his head with a smile and immediately Ahmed appointed him to be my hiking guide for the day.

As Mustafa approached to shake my hand, I saw his sweet duvet of vellus hair growing above the upper lip and out the sides of his nose. A slim eighteen-year-old with bulging mountainous muscles in the legs, he started out quick into the gorge and I struggled to keep up. He took his appointment seriously, silently at first.

We passed through the thick forest valley of soft fruits, almond, date palm and orange. All the houses were attached to each other in the tiny village on the other side. We took the narrow red road past a collective granary where two men stacked jute bags of barley. Arrived at the family home for tea, olives, and warm khubz dipped in argan oil, Mustafa's little brother, sisters, mother and grandmother for company. We ate together while listening to Michael Jackson's *Thriller* on cassette.

Stuffed ourselves with the good bread, then by early afternoon headed out into the sun and rough terrain where sheep and climbing goats showed better dexterity than I. We hiked for hours in the valley bed, the sun hitting our backs while, ahead of us, the gateway to the gorge opened its soaring walls three hundred feet high above the rugged rock pass. No souls in sight as the path narrowed to just one foot across. Sheer cliffs rose high on either side, millions of years compacted into red lime and sandstone.

We took a break to smoke kif and drink water. Passed the sebsi between us in silence with private thoughts running so quick around our heads that we couldn't speak. There was a palpable force between us heightened by the silence. Then, right beside me on the ground, a cracked open geode exposing its crystalline pink hollow. Excited, we began throwing rock against rock wall to see if any more precious minerals lay inside. A window opened between us and everything was allowed to mix together. We found more geodes and unusual black stones that Mustafa did not recognize. Filled our pockets as the sun lowered its head behind the High Atlas.

Once back at the beginning, Mustafa and I lay out our treasures on the counter and Ahmed was clearly pleased. "These are for you," we both said.

"You found treasure, *Mashallah*!" he exclaimed, looking closely at the stones. Picking up a black one, he examined it for some time, "But these ones are pieces of meteorite. You found rocks from heaven, sister. I can't take them, they are valuable."

I refused. Ahmed left the room. He returned and set five crystals down on the countertop, each a bright coloured orb its own force. I picked one up, aragonite—a translucent orange bomb in mid-explosion. Vanadinite had blood red hexagon crystals jeweled into rock, red dragon quartz, pink candy calcite and mild desert rose. All treasure.

"These are for you," said Ahmed. "Some are from the Sahara and others, from the Atlas. The guest is a gift from God." And all the day was crystalline.

Mustafa had disappeared by the time Ahmed brought out a bottle of fig liqueur, and we raised our glass. I asked him what question he had posed to his sons earlier in Tamazight.

He laughed. "I knew they would all want to accompany a beautiful woman on a hike in the mountains, so I asked each of them to give some account of their laziness. Habib answered that he was so intuitive about the human being that he barely needed to lift a finger, then Siddiq said that he could know someone by sheer compulsion. But Mustafa simply smiled. He did the least to transmit to me his desire to spend time with you. He harvested without even ploughing."

"I don't understand."

"It means, you take care of your business and let Allah take care of Allah's business. These two wings work together to make the bird fly."

# The Gatekeeper

NEXT DAY THERE WAS A small caravan heading east
to Sahara; it was led by a broad-shouldered man with
silver hair at the temples and a thick, luxuriant beard.
He had a hearty laugh as he approached and bowed.
Something about him magnetic, commanding.

"*As-salamu alaykum, je m'appelle Ali.*" His hand on
his heart, he smiled and his brown eyes opened wide,
peaceful and full of luster. "Come," said Ali, "I'll take you
to the desert."

We jolted up and down for hours in the jeep on
rough, sun-cracked terrain. The road was arduous,
perspiratory and dense. Ali barely spoke a word to his
companion or the two French tourists and me in the
back seat. I asked if he had been born in the desert.

"I have been bringing people into *alsahra'* for many years. I used to be more active in my community, but now I live slowly. Carry messages from the town to the desert and back again. Spend time with my family, work on the farm. Dig wells. I'm good at locating water. *It's never the value of water but thirst.*"

We had left the mountains for flat, roadless, black hamada. The horizon soon became nothing. By late afternoon we had reached Kasbah le Touareg in Merzouga. A refurbished cube in the middle of horizontal earth, a tiny fortress against the massive Erg Chebbi sand dune behind it—first glimpse of Sahara's edge. You've got to be brave to wear black in the desert.

Our bags unloaded, I mentioned that I would walk around the village to find the kasbah that someone had recommended.

Without warning, Ali's temper took fire, "There are rooms in THIS hotel for everyone! It's not expensive AT ALL for tourists!"

He picked up my backpack and headed toward Le Touareg. I ran and took it from him. He seized my arm.

"I did not bring you all this way for nothing. Not everyone is allowed into the desert! This is the city of knowledge. These are not enemy lands, sister," as he released my arm. "Trust me. What you are seeking is right in front of you. There is nothing else nearby. This is a good place."

"*Eyvallah*," said a voice from the other side of the story.

Later, once the intensity of the day had subsided, I joined the French couple for a late afternoon walk. The temperature was plunging and the breeze whipped sand in our faces as we followed the trail of tire tracks down to the dunes. Ali and his companions joined in and persuaded us over to Dayet Srij, a glassy lake of rainwater. Often a dry bed, it was today a sprawling expanse. In the dream distance, the massive amber Erg Chebbi dune reflected in it.

Miraculous slender-necked flamingos with pink bodies and feathers dipped in fire and ash appeared. We moved in closer to the one-leggeds, black and blood-red wings lifting a heavy body. But union easy. Levitation, one of the five Sufi powers. Original whirling dervishes of the natural world. We gave thanks to Ali, who was truly adept at finding water.

Heading back now, he guided us into the empty village where a carpet seller awaited our arrival. We were unable to escape. Ali was visibly annoyed by our lack of purchasing power.

Late that night, I sat on the upper terrace under the ephemeral stars. There were jumping camel spiders and low-flying, carnivorous, long-eared bats nesting in the crevices of the kasbah. I lit some kif to ease the tension and Ali approached with his friends. We shared the kif and Ali joked.

"The Sahara Desert drifts into a bar. What does the bartender say?" He paused. "Long time no sea!" Everybody laughed. Soon after came talk of riding camels in the dunes at sunrise next day—for a hefty price. I declined. Ali persisted. I disappeared.

The alarm sounded at half past four in the morning and I jumped out of a sweltering sleep to greet the Absolute.

Walked straight out the back door into dune. Climbed up silent, immobile at the top of flashing peaks of sand as the sun gave *As-salam*. Rambled up the crest of higher dunes even. Algerian border just up ahead forty clicks. Desert dust gave me a proper whipping. Standing, seated or resting diagonal on a dune, she caught me. Crystals and fossils jutting out of the smooth cinnamon banks.

The sun rose and pushed me and my mild melanin out the way. Back in the room, I removed my underwear and a cup of Sahara fell to the ground from between my legs. The Absolute is always with you.

When I descended for breakfast, I saw Ali there with his companions. Overwhelmed by his presence, I knew I had to leave. They told me that public transport no longer ran from Merzouga. Ali was the only driver available to take me to the next town—for a price. The gatekeeper had me with the strength of a rock.

I left at noon for Erfoud and the French couple joined the ride. Ali drove us again in silence. Out the window, the decaying corpse of a dromedary came into view by the side of the stark road. I threw it a prayer. The prayer was returned.

In Erfoud, we each paid our portion. Suddenly, Ali said that thirty dirham was missing. As we argued, a crowd of taxi drivers congregated around us. It was a campaign against financial corruption and unfair tourist privileges, a disparity cry, a self-accounting.

"*C'est beaucoup d'argent pour un marocain mais pas pour un touriste.*" It's a lot of money for a Moroccan but not for a tourist.

We surrendered. An hour later I was sitting at the back of a bus headed to Errachidia—dusty, barefoot and bleeding in Western clothes. That night, I heard Sufis chanting a *zikr* outside the hotel window as I smoked Marlboro after Marlboro sitting on the edge of the windowsill alone in the room.

*La ilaha illallah, La ilaha illallah, La ilaha illallah, La ilaha illallah, La ilaha illallah,* someone knocked at the door, *ilaha illallah, La ilaha illallah, La ilaha illallah, La ilaha illallah,* when I answered, *ilaha illallah,* there was no one there, *ilaha illallah, La ilaha illallah,* I returned to the window, *ilaha illallah, La ilaha illallah,* but the *zikr* had ceased.

# Four

Love is fire, love is fire.

–Hz. Ahmad al-Rifa'i

# The Scent of Cedar

IN THE MIDDLE OF MIDDLE ATLAS Mountains, in the centre of central Azrou, a town a thousand and one metres high, in high-thirties July heat. A scorching summer of afternoon sunburns. No travellers here but me, and I blend.

*"Est-ce que tu crois en Dieu?"* Do you believe in God? asked the man from the other side of the story.

*"Je ne suis pas Musulmane."* I am not Muslim.

*"Est-ce que tu crois en Dieu?"* Do you believe in God?

*"Oui."* Yes.

*"Donc, tu es croyante."* Then, you are a believer.

Azrou is a rock worthy of pilgrimage, a well-hidden, well-revealed village sanctuary. From a corner inside Le Café des Cèdres, I looked out onto large open windows at the backs of men sitting in pairs, as they looked out onto the sun-drenched Place Mohammed V. They sat immobile with smoke rising from their rounded, easygoing bodies. I hid indoors. Broken coffee on the white tablecloth. A glass of clear water. The aged butterscotch pages of Rimbaud's *Poésies* in hand. This edition inscribed to someone named Mohamed.

*"C'est la vie encore! Plus tard, les délices de la damnation seront plus profondes. Un crime, vite, que je tombe au néant, de par la loi humaine,"* says Rimbaud in *Saison en enfer*. It's still Life! Later, the delights of damnation will run deeper. A crime, quick, may I fall to nothingness, by human law.

When the book released me for a moment, I noticed that the café had filled. Among the arrivals, a man sitting alone reading a book in a nearby blind spot, I didn't catch him at first, but I felt the eyes. Time elastic.

He waved. Waved again. Walked over and asked if I, by any chance, had a book to exchange. In his outstretched hand, *Le Pain Nu,* by Mohamed Choukri. Ha! Instinct said leave it alone. *Quel instinct pourri!*

Mourad was a thirty-six-year-old man in a child's body, cheeks plump with baby fat on a delicate, small-boned frame with a mess of loose black curls about the head. A spark of Black Africa in his Arabic tones. He was soft-spoken and intelligent, but entrenched in a firm belief in God as an entity outside of himself, on that we disagreed. This transient fervour was both a discredit and a downfall.

He enticed me into hiking the cedar forest on the extinct volcanic craters outside of town. We took a quick *grand* taxi and everything turned calm as we entered the trees. The muffled shrieks of faraway Barbary macaques and nearby birdsong. The scent of cedar hit our noses like sex.

Mourad and I moved deeper into the forest without taking notice of the distant dogs approaching slow and secretive in attack position. Suddenly, three-headed beasts with sheer, flashing eyes leapt out all at once with violent barking. We bent to pick up stones in our defence, pretended to throw—they retreated. Three tongues receded back into the forest, whimpering.

I never know, but I go. Leave the known for the unknown. Possible violence. Possible death. For those on the margins, it is always the season of the wild dog. Once in the jaws of predators, the victim may appear to go into deep shock. Within a few minutes, the prey is dismembered. The dogs gorge themselves to fill their bellies. Even the mother takes a piece of the hunt. Regurgitates it. Pups clamour to receive their share.

Mourad and I walked for hours in the searing sun on a path lined with fields of red poppy. Conversation came easy, but when we sat to rest, the suitor revealed himself. The tongue did its duty and I gently declined his advances. He persisted. The deciduous forest had struck him like an aphrodisiac.

*"On se tient la main?"* he asked in the perfumed woods, as the branches broke underfoot. Shall we hold hands?

*"Mais monsieur, mes yeux parlaient simplement d'amitié. Je suis une sorcière mais ce n'est que par accident, je vous le jure!"* But sir, my eyes spoke only of friendship. I'm a witch but it is only by accident, I swear!

*La* means no in Arabic. The sound is both muse and music to the sixth sense. But how many times can the word *no* be negated? *La ilaha illallah.*

Leave all other notions behind you, my friend. They are best kept buried in the communal palace of unknowing. Woman alone never made such a fuss again and again and again.

# Matityahu

WE RETURNED TO AZROU in early evening as the wind drew a cool, double-edged sword down over the Rif. The moment we entered Le Café des Cèdres, a tall, skinny, European-looking man rose to greet us. Young, handsome, disheveled, a full head of chestnut mess, he held out a slender hand and introduced himself as Matthieu, a poet from Tiohtià:ke/Montréal, my hometown.

After coffee, Matthieu led the way past the cinema, down through the winding maze of the medina with its unadorned buildings hiding great temples inside. We came to a dilapidated, green door that opened onto a courtyard living room inside Matthieu's rich, derelict palace. Stuccoed, peeling, yellow walls forever and vibrant red door frames rising high around us meeting at a sunroof of glass. A kitchen to one side, two bedrooms on the other. The floor tilework was a psychedelic green, black and gold mosaic.

We each took a seat on pillows around the wine table, octagonal and low. Our faces illuminated by candlelight now. Carved iron lanterns, endless Marlboros and bad Sauvignons. Matthieu's baby-blue portable typewriter on the floor in the corner, which he had named *Dounia*, meaning *world*. Wine and discourse opened a door between us all in the geometric centre of the inner courtyard. Damn these meetings with surprising men and endless bottles of red.

Matthieu smothered us in stories as Mourad and I sat wide-eyed like young children around the fire when the storyteller speaks about that time he and a friend drove up from New York City to Quebec and crossed the U.S.-Canada border at Champlain with thirty thousand dollars cash hidden in the trunk. Or how he would smoke joints with his father before going out to play hockey on the frozen lake in upstate New York. Or how his brother-in-law was the family pusher for all the aunts and uncles. His father was the only exception because he grew his own organics behind the house.

"Life can be so soft when we forget for a few hours the universe of things. So wonderful to concentrate on vision and senses at the centre of a flux never interrupted by thought or impressions. In the end we try to live in harmony for a few hours, or at least see the beauty," said Matthieu before the final *al-'isha azan* of the night. We all fell quiet for a moment, listening. Who called me here? I am a beast, a monster of sadness. I cannot pass this on to others. I should leave now.

Just then a spark from the candle hit an open book on the table. It was a bright red softcover of the *Bardo Thödol*. The flare exposed an echo of love, a curvature of muscle, filament of bone, bruised vena cava, the poet's jawline, Matthieu's great literature of Mind. Alive, I began to burn. Poetry takes poets to poets.

The dome of sleep came then and Matthieu offered Mourad and I each a bed for the night. We knew that there was a palpable need to make this bond persist through the method of our actions.

I prostrated myself into dream. There, Shams had thrown himself from a building and fallen onto the ground. He lay flat and bleeding on his stomach but was not dead. He raised himself slightly.

"My heart."

"Here, take mine," I said, kneeling.

He put his hand to his chest and died. His body had not been damaged, only the heart had broken.

Next day, Matthieu invited me to move in with him. Boots afoot and shawl to the wind, I escaped early morning, whore-like, gliding down the alley where storekeepers rubbed sleep out of their eyes and took note of my passing.

## Rimbaud, Mon Amour

AT TIMES YOU ARRIVE ONLY to leave without leaving an impression. At others, you change direction quickly, and instead of heading into morning, you answer an invitation from the Friend. At that moment robed men offer me cigarettes from the balcony of their rented room as I check out of l'Hotel des Cèdres and move in with Matthieu.

We prepare. We are never prepared. A beautiful shame to want the solitude that only another foreign writer can offer.

This, as Mourad tells me that I have moved him, moved his heart. He is a fine student of life, full of desire, but the poet has charm in their hair alone. And Matthieu is a poet of all youth, all wisdom.

"*À bas la forme littéraire! Aujourd'hui je n'ai pas envie d'écrire mais j'ai envie d'être avec toi—*ENVIE. *Dans envie, il y a Vie!*" shouts Matthieu. Down with literary form! Today I don't want to write, I want to be with you— WANT. In wanting, there is Life! "You are a great woman, beautiful, fascinating, believe it! I swear I wish there were more women like you, the world would be a little less cruel. I love you already from all points of view."

Should I adore him simply because he loves me so suddenly? What am I doing here? Is this the fate of the wandering woman of a certain age? And what do we think of these young idolaters? I have only one urgency, and it is, without a doubt, the opposite of that of the crowd.

"Old man," I say in my deepest rasp, "Can I smoke on your rooftop? I want to write and let go of some clothing."

"Of course my dear, but first show me your breasts," he smirks.

At the end of the day, the sun summoned my desire for Matthieu, despite my sorrow. Swelled my sex like yeasted dough, proving itself. Mouth full, our groins hard, pages darkened, hearts ashened, spirits in air, tender sex ours for the having and the walls moist with it.

"I want you. Your drive, to feel it, I want you to be aroused."

This kneading and punching lasted for hours. To release the air through moaning. To roll and cut before falling into hot oil. Each step an important part of the cookery. After the meal, we smoked kif before falling asleep.

Next day, I sprang up from the mattress on the floor, the taste of small death on the lips. These voyages frighten. Help me, *Rimbaud, mon amour.*

*"Je suis sûr que je suis plus intéressant que Rimbaud,"* declares Matthieu. I'm sure I'm much more interesting than Rimbaud.

# Poet's Poet

On the yellow living room wall, Matthieu had put up black and white postcards of Allen Ginsberg and Bob Dylan at a party in 1965 and Amiri Baraka back when he was still LeRoi Jones. This was our continuum of poets. I took this to be a blessing on our endeavours. Shams now pushed to the back of Mind, impatiently waiting, rabid. Spearmint tea, hunger and lust now renewed interests. The fit of mouths, the soft and solid between the legs. Who gave this poet the right to fall inside me so quick?

"I sometimes get hard while I'm writing," says Matthieu one afternoon like nothing. "And then, in my mind, I tell myself that I am a great writer. I can do it. The greatest writer in the world who could succeed in getting someone aroused through words, wet from start to finish through poetic coaxing alone."

Ha! But to have such a riotous lover—even for a moment. Our mouths both dry from anxiety, wine and Western pharmaceuticals threatening to calm our breakouts. Together, we make one Janus. One body, one head, two faces. He takes antipsychotic medication to calm the hallucinations. I trashed all my pills in Miami and now reap the inflammatory results. Do not let it scare you, I say to myself. Let it be a welcome guest, like a gift from God.

"The most recent diagnosis," Matthieu unveils one morning, "is that I was classified as schizophrenic with a significant delay in development on several levels, social in particular. So, I can't understand how a woman like you could take interest in a man like me. I don't want to believe; I want to understand. For me, it's easy to say I'm crazy actually, but explaining why I'm crazy is another matter altogether. Explain to me why you're with me," he demands, cracking open his first beer at noon. "I don't know, maybe I'm just predisposed to psychosis."

With Matthieu, the discourses were sometimes short and lightning like a Gulf Stream crossing, or lengthy and painful with the corporeal ravaged like the face of Burroughs or Bukowski with their combined hundred years of work under the belt. Veins on the nose, cheeks sunken like boats attempting a crossing—unsuccessful. Wrinkles the only waves left. Bags of skeletons on the Styx, but what Poetry! A knowledge rendered Absolute and Explosive. A molecule of *Nur* in all the pages.

I just want to be alone with you, a return customer scared of her own reflection. You make me slightly weak in the knees. I am transformed at higher speed than normal.

We edge the fantastic but it is a long and guarded border. The weight of water, the spirit located, the death of God, Unity of God—two writers should not take up residence and expect to get anything but work done. The work and the living become wholly inseparable. There is such an equal exchange that the writing can barely capture a moment before another arises with such intensity!

*"Ce n'est pas la forme, c'est l'essence qui m'intéresse,"* says Matthieu. It is not the form, it is the essence that interests me.

We make a single sound. Each a last and final prayer. Our solar plexus on the sleeve. Invocation when both speaking and speechless. The Song of Strong Sun.

*"Tu gouttes la cigarette et la poésie,"* he whispers, kissing a lobe. You taste of cigarettes and poetry.

A little solitude before the fire, please. Such elegant anticipation when nothing is as sacred or as profound as this. I pray neither of us runs out of oxygen. I am not ready to finish my breath practices yet.

# Herb Afrik

As QUICKLY AS I LAND, I take off. Breaking open our bubble after two weeks inside. Unwrap myself from Azrou's arms and like a good traveller, gather all my belongings and leave at dawn. A yawning Matthieu walks me to the bus. Abandonment is real.

I hug desert lowland, High Atlas in the distance and ten hours later narrow red alleys scented with amber open before me. Faith around every corner. Marrakesh is a layered touchstone, *amur akush* the Land of God. Noise and chaos, a show or a slow, robed walk on the hot edge of death—easy. Seductive. Impossible even to imagine the sustain. The high-pitched music. The five times prayer. A woman's head covered tight for days.

I run away to my old friends Solitude, Ablution and Toiletries. My vanity no less, part conditioning, part condition. At sunset, I climb onto the rooftop terrace of Hotel Afriquia to smoke kif. It is deserted except for occasional palm and the *clack clack* of giant storks courting each other from nests five stories high. The *azan*, nothing more—all actions suspended as the praise song comes at me from minarets on all sides.

After one night in Marrakesh the road takes me deeper south to Essaouira again. Once there, I head straight to the souk and Hakim who greets me with a knowing smile and royal mint, rose and opium tea. I had run into the arms of another man.

Our nerves calm after a few sips, Hakim sits close to tell me about the Sufi brotherhood of the Gnawa. His ancestors were neither literate nor original speakers of Arabic, but slaves brought from sub-Saharan West Africa. The legacy of African animism and Sufism lives on through the ceremony of poetry, music and dance known as the *lila*.

"In the *lila*, we invoke the Invisible. We recall the experiences of our ancestors. Praise them and the unity of all that is. It is an act of absolution, forgiveness and gratitude. Your timing is perfect, my sister. The festival begins tonight."

This is why I had come.

After a strong cup of touba coffee spiced with guinea pepper and clove, our energies increased. Hakim closed the shop and we headed out into the streets where nothing was forced. He held my hand for a time, then disappeared, then I disappeared. Both of us hidden inside the festival of perfect and missed encounters. This was the world Shams had tried to show me.

Like a lightning madwoman, ideas crossed my mind, invaded me, then left. They would not cease. I was in the thick of the audience now. The hypnotic frequencies of the music enhanced the communal trance. The crowd thick and swaying as one in time with the rhythm. No such thing as direction. Only the low-tones of the sintir bass accented by high iron krakeb castanets and Arabic prayers sung in call and response over and over. *La ilaha illallah.* The whole of it an invocation. Love ritualized. A bringing together of communal needs into One. A natural sense of belonging on African soil. Ceremonial reminders of divine living. Desire increased and quenched. A return to the source. The inside of the chest. The arms. The air. Lift. Light. *Nurun Ala Nur.* Is this how conversions begin?

# Presence and Abandonment

I RETURN TO MATTHIEU three days later—no—it was he who found me lost in the middle of Boulevard Moulay Abdelkader, sick and bruised from the festival. He put his arm around me and we stumbled to Paradise Café where avocado milk was the precise remedy. I had been emptied by Hakim's medicine and the gathering of Friends. Azrou's medina rang loud around us, and Matthieu, *Le Bateau ivre*, was trying hard to save me from myself. He brought me home, bathed me, prepared the tea, and embedded me.

*"Tu m'aimes pour mon chagrin tandis que je m'allonge en pleurant, folle d'opium, même. L'amour prend fin et recommence simultanément. Sans raison, ni but. Une simple action vécue sans pensée. Je m'infiltre sans vouloir m'infiltrer,"* I tell him. You love me for my sorrow while I lay here weeping, mad with opium, even. Love ends and begins simultaneously without reason or purpose. A simple act lived without thought. I implicate myself without motive.

We both needed saving in this sacred and secular story. When I wake up next morning, I offer myself to him only because he had not yet begun to drink that day. But alcohol is a poet's blood, you don't escape it that easy. You leave it from time to time for drugs or lovemaking, but always return to intoxication.

He had wanted me to leave the bathroom door open after lovemaking so we would never be apart. Perhaps he had simply wanted to protect me and I was grateful for that. But where was the freedom for either of us? For my own security, I closed the door. I could only give so much. We argued and it set us both to writing. Strange, this writing in the Presence. It is a binding freedom. We are close, living each day just shy of happiness.

Even now, in the throes of writing next to each other on the floor beneath the bright, late-day sun, I leave Matthieu's side and move to the rooftop for solitude.

"*Tu m'abandonnes encore*," he pleads. You're abandoning me again.

"*Oui, mon amour.*"

Love always asks something of the future.

# Waking and Dreaming

THE LINE BETWEEN WAKING and dreaming disappears. I am meeting people in dreams that I have met in previous dreams and discussing this inside the dream itself. An invisible reality presents without fail. Which one which? Do not resist life, it says.

In this dream, I am preparing breakfast. A man whom I understand to be my husband tries to help, but fails. I scold him. Pouring hot cardamom tea through a jute napkin is not a good idea when one is still half-dreaming. He retreats to folding laundry, sighs and looks out the eastern window as the morning pours in, bathing him in sunlight. I place steaming tea before him.

Just then, three men walk by outside in the street carrying a black cloth with something heavy in it. One of them is the man who will become my *murshid*. I call out but no one hears. All I can think is, *get your things and go to them*. But I wake up instead—dry-mouthed, thinking, *why didn't I help them carry that stone?*

# Prayer Positions

TRANSITIONAL SMOOTH, the light does eventually come. These legs fold easy now. Lotus a natural prayer position. Trance comes at odd times though. The key to a solid meditation is not moving, though I moved to tell you this.

The sun veils. Matthieu has been asleep for sixteen hours. It's his medication—*les épées empoisonnées*. Better to trust the African pharmacy, so I burn white benzoin to deepen our disposition, settle myself into position on the terrace and welcome the *al-zuhr* call to prayer. A meditation overtakes to join both love and death into one act or non-act.

In Zen, you are taught to sit still in lotus with eyes half open and focus on breathing. In Vipassanā, you observe consciousness at the edge of a nostril, and let it swim freely about until a strong pulse can take it helix-like up the thigh or down the scalp at will. In Tasawwuf, discourse on Truth, Love, dreams and human beings are communal. Meditation can be silent, seated, sung, swayed, chanted, turned, and is always held in service. Ecstatic prayer as practice for living. It comes from inspiration and runs toward unity, *Tawhid*. There are ceremonies and then there are the source of ceremonies. It is a question of remembering.

Blessings on the men who perform ablutions and pray outside our window.

"How do you pray?" one asks me from his chair as I pass beside the mosque on my way to market. "We raise our hands cupping our palms together like begging bowls to ask and receive. How do you pray?"

"It's personal," I say and run quickly away.

As I cross our door sill with groceries in hand, Matthieu emerges from the bedroom shirtless with his notebook in hand, "I would really like to write something on Nina Simone and women of the South, but strangely enough I cannot put into words what I feel for them. It would be easier with music, but I'm not a musician. So fuck it, I pray. I pray for you too love, my dear. I send you constant energy with all sincerity."

I set the bags down and embrace him. The tears come again. I am doing this, but really, I don't know how to do this. Take refuge, leave refuge. Prayer is the inner medicine for outward action. Repeat the names of God. You'll excuse me, sometimes I want to pay more attention to the unity of God.

# The Brilliance

Every day, the poet cloaks himself in black and goes out for broken coffee to remember civilian life. He is a man living only in spirit to the detriment of the body. Ascetic outside of opium tea, kif, vodka, Volubilia red and *café cassé au Paradis*.

I am praying now, learning the Fatiha interrupted only by his goodbye kiss before he steps out into the medina. This I accept, but for him to have forgotten his dreams—that I do not!

He withdraws and I rush to clean, eat and smoke so quickly that I burn my lip. The fire is ready. I accept that I need help. I light a fire out of my hair. The brilliance! I need not move to have union with God or be awake to God. Stillness is key. Stop for a second damn it!

Just then, Matthieu returns home to catch me off guard.

This time, I am shirtless, sweeping the floor, a half-smoked Marlboro dangling from the left side and dreadlocked hair in defiance of all gravity. I wipe the sweat from my brow knowing this body is scarred beyond recognition. I have voluntarily moved into the shade. Consumption itself needs a purge. A purge toward the Truth is a good idea. I see now, there is Beauty, even in death, even in my inabilities. In my failures with Shams, there is Light.

# Tavern of Two Doors

"*ELLE EST FOLLE DE TA FOLIE, et tu es fou d'elle,*" says Sabour each time he visits us for afternoon wine. She is crazy for your madness and you are crazy for her.

Sabour, Mourad, Aadil and Abbas were becoming regular customers at the house. I suspected Muslims in disguise who had a misunderstanding of wine-rapture from all their inebriated nights until dawn.

One time, I had left the living room party early to write, leaving the men to their red drink and football debate over Atlas Lions versus Blues. Once in the next room, I had nothing to put down. I drank vodka like water, afraid of my own swollen sex.

Perhaps I am here for the Beloved to come and collect me. Walk, walk, my Love. Your very step gives me sign of submission. I am drunk in the tavern, but is it the right one? I am on a boat crossing the Styx. In a room with a view of ruins. Barely present in this room.

Next morning a deafening crash rouses me from bed. I open the bedroom door and see Abbas lying on the living room floor on his back, awkward, immobile, eyes wide open staring up at the sunroof. His deeply lined, copper-skinned face offers no reflection. A chest of lid, jutting teeth, mouth open with frothing pink vomit leaking off the right side. I grab his hand and touch the wrist, the neck, looking for a pulse. But there is none. He is dead.

In truth, he is not dead at all, only dead drunk. Died in the living room after the kind of night where good men refuse good food in order to intoxicate themselves further into violent unconsciousness. The glass of cheap red put up to the test of ensuing nausea, vomit and the shit of the Depressed.

"*Ouf, il y a des matins où ça fait mal et des crépuscules qui donnent envies de rire—en tout cas j'ignore où je vais épuiser toute cette énergie, je n'ai pas peur JE N'AI PAS PEUR,*" says Matthieu. There are mornings where it hurts and evenings that make you want to laugh—anyway I don't know where I'm going to use up all this energy, but I'm not afraid I AM NOT AFRAID.

## Ville Nouvelle

AFTER THE INCIDENT with Abbas, Matthieu and I leave town for a while. We've been together forty days. The vintage *grand* taxi holds us for two hours, collecting strangers by the side of the road, until the dust of Fes rises up around us.

On the white colonial streets, men walk holding hands affectionately but tap Matthieu on the shoulder when he kisses me defiantly at the crosswalk. The medina is medieval and time exists beside itself, outside of space and causality.

Near the city centre, we find a weathered, velvet restaurant that serves alcohol to men sitting in their own thick smoke as sun washes through the stained-glass window. I am the only woman in the bar with a boy who needs to be saved from himself. What good can come of this?

*"Je n'echapperai rien, je ne laisserai rien au hasard—tu excuseras le biffage, okay? Et tu excuseras tout ce qu'il pourrait y avoir à excuser. Merci,"* says Matthieu. I will not escape anything, I will not leave anything to chance—you will excuse anything I've left out, okay? And I apologize for anything that needs an apology. Thank you.

A black cat comes and goes. Is it a sign? We have seen this before. What am I doing here with this man who lives only in his mind? The body long lost to acts of human stress repetition, devoured by its own spirit tenant. He is no good to me in bed these days, but good—a good human being. Will I abandon him the way Shams abandoned me? Relive the end of my previous affair only to have the roles reversed? Why in the land of God did Shams leave me?

## Strong Will to Make
## Flames Appear

The call to prayer vanishes in this loud modern mess of Fes. The newspaper reports that a muezzin fainted after calling yesterday's *al-asr*. It is remarkable that he did not die in this summer heat.

I'm an old fart at thirty—flawed, scarred and sagging. Mirrors compliment me on my use of gravity. I'm still trying to relate to the aging process as it manifests. This muscle pulled easy, that silver pubic hair. Even the scent between my legs has changed. A coarse inland sea salt wet from attempts at ceaseless prayer. The whole house smells of umami, Volubilia red, shit and sexual endeavours—could be bad for the kidneys.

Suddenly, a strange symptom occurs, a burning, though not for human delights but for all that is. For the secret inside all the events of the world.

These days you need strong will just to make flames appear. If I stay here, I will be destroyed along with Matthieu. Die a slow death with this young man too drunken and skeletal to look up from his scribblings.

Hooded like a child or a prophet, he slips past our hotel doors and into the souk for Marquises and bottles of Volubilia. In the end, we both take our poison with allegiance and privacy. Never forget the value of intoxication in the big city. I couldn't see his voice, you see. His voice made love to me. It hit me fully with the Voice of Voices. The Giant Embrace.

It is clear that Matthieu is not the end result but part of the organic process. I take refuge in him because in my state, there are still too many aggressors around, visible even from this luxurious, medieval Fes windowsill.

That afternoon, I hear the lighter snap beside my ear as I sit in silence, breathing. Eyes open quick. I think Matthieu might set fire to my skin. His lighter, close to my cheek. I gasp. He kisses me full on the mouth. Wet and lust. O the volatility of love. If I go up in flames, so be it.

# Awe

As soon as we return to Azrou, Matthieu and Mourad talk about me behind my back over coffee in Paradise. My ears burn from down the street and all I can think to do is leave. My turn to sacrifice now. No expectations save for what is, and what is created by putting one foot in front of the other.

When they return home, a small fist fight erupts between them. I break it apart. Madness. I struggle and my underwear is soaking wet. There is no denying what natural love brings forth from both these human beings. Discourse, discord, orgasm, and awe.

An empty hallway is suddenly full—no—what already exists becomes manifest. Two eyes see the power of one action, visible and invisible. *Comme dans les tempêtes de sable, il faut se momifier pour passer à travers. Il faut être plus feu qu'elle.* Like an oncoming sandstorm, one must mummify oneself in order to pass through. One must become more fire than her.

*Une profonde méditation me tombe tout droit de l'au-delà.* A deep meditation falls straight down from the beyond.

*Une boucle de puissance fluide. Les limites du corporel vite dépassées. Vaincues avec Toi.* A fluid buckle of power. Limits of the body quickly exceeded. Defeated with You.

*Je n'y vois rien dans ce noir. Mais je n'ai aucun choix, seulement un devoir. Ma vue s'éclaircit lentement. Le ciel est privé de nuages. Je plane.* I see nothing in this dark. But I have no choice, only a duty. The view is slowly clearing. The sky is wanting of clouds. I am soaring.

*Je vis mon avenir à chaque instant. Je n'oublie pas l'éternel.* I live my own fate at every moment. I do not forget the eternal.

*L'éclat divin me donne mal au coeur et ma vision se lance à travers tout ce qui est solide. Je suis solide et donc je vois à travers moi-même.* The divine burst makes me sick to my stomach and my vision throws itself through everything that is solid. I am solid and therefore see through myself.

*Je n'ai pas envie de courir mais de marcher lentement, avec légèreté, le temps d'apprécier ma nouvelle vision. Je suis un peu myope, mais de près, quels moments!* I have no desire to run but rather to walk slow, with grace, taking the time to appreciate this new astonishment. I am somewhat short-sighted, but up close, what moments!

Matthieu means Matityahu, gift from Yahweh, gift from God. And he loves me! An assuredly mad soul. I am not tired, my love, *mais épanouie.*

# The Battle of Exiles

Today the house is thundering with voices arguing louder than Charlie Parker's horn. Just goes to confirm that it's not yet time to visit the world where two brothers war. Matthieu and Mourad yell about me in the living room again. Fighting words and bebop. I seclude myself with headphones in the bedroom. Mourad slams the door on his way out and Matthieu comes to me, stands in the threshold, his face so young, radiant, exposed, emotional, sober for a quick moment. In the quiet, there is only Bird holding harmony and tempo like a sword.

"I love Mourad. I love him, I love him the way I love you—I would not want to be asked to choose between the two of you, I would be extremely annoyed. But God spares me this kind of pain, I'm grateful. Thank you," says Matthieu.

He challenges me to write more than him. But it's not a competition. I did not choose to write, saturated by this exorcism on paper that leads to nothing. This writing will not save anyone. A praise song from a madwoman to a madman and the man who left her. Ha! Matthieu be praised! He absconds with my heart. What can I do but give it?

"I wrote a quatrain for you but I'm too embarrassed to show you. In the end, it's nothing sensational, probably because each line has been thought and rethought and so there is an obvious lack of spontaneity, I am aware of it—I intend to review all my poems in order to get closer to balance."

We are high performance, all-terrain hunger, all day long into night. Dynamic. Intrepid. Nude regardless of clothing. Sex regardless of sex. But this is not my goal, my function remains to write, badly even. Therein lies the battle.

*"Il ne faut pas chercher à être poète, il faut l'être, ou ne pas l'être,"* dit Sabour, *le grand clochard qui boit comme un trou. C'est un drôle d'oiseau qui n'est pas toujours très drôle.* You cannot try to be a poet, you either are one, or you are not, says Sabour, the tramp who can't hold his drink. He's a funny bird who is not always very funny.

But the ego won't let go of me. It warps everything. Even the body politic—un-covered, un-perfumed, un-deodorized, un-washed, so apparent, so vulnerable.

"You're a peacock," says Matthieu to me in the mirror.

I'm dumbfounded again, agape. Can do nothing but observe my environment alongside grotesque intestinal gas emissions. I burp and it comes out *"Hamdullah."*

At moments like these, I don't even know whose face I'm looking into or whose eyes are looking out of this body.

Late one night, a thunder shakes the front door. Some-one pounds at us in a rage. Another drunk friend in the middle of night looking for wine, while we were in the heat of literary love.

It's Abbas. The one who had died drunk on the living room floor not long ago. He spits it all out for the medina to hear. Throws his vitriol at us while hitting the door for a quarter hour. Matthieu does not respond, nor do I. We sit in silence trying to write, ignoring the attack. Cats join in, howling like screaming children in the street.

"You have to leave Azrou gently," Abbas moans over and over in a drunken haze, "or we will make you leave. We will burn the building down."

Matthieu finally opens the door. I can hear compliant sounds but Abbas' voice intensifies before it abates again. They make their way into peace but I don't know how. After a few minutes we return quietly to the exile of our journals, side by side.

In the Presence, there is no such thing as solitude, although even friends may throw their embers. We sit in such a way so as to be closer to our own folded legs, Matthieu and I, scribbling away in the shattered night. Mostly calm after the fighting. Feet now hardened and powdered with Middle Atlas dust blown from the neighbour's terrace. Fresh-faced and sunken-eyed, torn-skinned and flexible even in the heat of hurt. We are guests, but am I being exiled from African soil?

"It's not a biography, it's a drunkography," says Matthieu without looking up from his writing.

# Opiates

OPIUM AND ALCOHOL CAN cause bloodletting but no one knows the extent of antipsychotics. Papaver pods induce relaxation through wild, vivid dreaming. It can take some time for the effects to appear. One must not overload the tea with seed. Crack five or six dry pods per small kettle. Just enough for possible inflamed pleasure and gratitude in all things.

We sit tight in our neuroses. Both of us crippled by the past, one that he cannot remember and one that I cannot forget. Results are the same.

One symptom of addiction to opium tea is a great itching upon the body. But this can be prevented by removing the seeds from the tea before drinking. Accept potential toxicity and expect certain levels of sickness, with fecal events and euphoric dreaming.

"*Mais j'ai le mal de l'univers, Maya. J'aimerais danser avec toi, naïve bulle de terre—ô bulle de feu en fait, qu'est ce qu'on ne pourrait pas encore inventer pour se tenir vivant,*" says Matthieu. But I'm sick of the universe, Maya. I just want to dance with you, naive bubble of earth—bubble of fire. What we could invent just the two of us in order to hold on to life.

Matthieu asks if he is the most spectacular man I have met in Morocco. I tell him that he is the only person I know well.

"*Je peux bien me passer de toi,*" he tells me. I can do without you.

"*Tant mieux.*" Whatever, I reply.

"*J'suis l'enfer.*" I'm the bomb, he says, smiling.

Later, he'll shrug his shoulders and throw me a childish look saying, "I love you."

We are part art and part medicine. Part dopamine blocker and isotretinoin. Morphine, codeine, noscapine, papaverine, thebaine, fat, protein, plant wax, latex, sugar and bitter grape.

I try to heal this man's manic depression with microdoses of opium, but I simply replace one drug with another. All this to dispel his desire for midday drunkenness and possible seizures by early afternoon.

"The psychiatrist appeared so insensitive when he spoke to me about my hypersensitivity. It's amazing that I can even contain so many hundreds of pills inside this febrile body," says Matthieu.

In a moment, we will cease decaying, *Inshallah*. Madness touches. We push it back. It is the game of the universe.

I am a failure today, ineffective. My incessant breathing leads to heavy legs and arms, paranoia, withdrawal, sadness, fear, insomnia, uncertainty, fatigue, acid reflux, back pain, pimples, Fatihas, drunkenness, turning, sitting, writing and a longing for what was never really mine.

I examine my face in the bathroom mirror. Today again my lips and cupid's bow are all red and throbbing, tomorrow the skin will crack and fall away. Side effects. All my muscles sore, coordination off. Our libidos dry from drugs. Our bodies in the end, one two-headed bird attempting to fly with varying degrees of failure.

One morning as we lay lazy in bed, Matthieu told me about the last sexual encounter he'd had before we met. It had been four months earlier, for money, but he had refused to pay. In the end he did, but the act had disgusted him. His ambiguous relationship with sex caused much of his suffering and anguish. Most of it due to the side effects of the medication.

"*Ça mène à quoi à la fin? C'est quoi cette énergie sexuelle qui nous domine, qui nous possède, qui nous tient à ses pieds mais nom de Dieu je n'y comprendrai jamais rien.*" What is it all for in the end? What is this sexual energy that dominates us, possesses us, has us by the throat, in the name of God I will never understand anything.

In my bleakness, my organ shrinks. People fall in love with me and again it swells. What is this living? In the end, it is easy to love someone, but difficult for the other person to love themselves or give what little remains.

## Prelude to Liberation

Show yourself, young elder. Reveal your list of geniuses, your desires refused. Your sex grows hard when you write, and when you read your writing. With my face between your thighs and your writers' hands in my locked hair, we will one day be free of all derision—*promis, juré*—I swear. Let us drink the horrible wine of Azrou, smoke the kif and take the ink and lead in hand and all-natural delirium by the ass to vanquish this fantastic suffering. Task impossible. Task unforgettable.

Rise! I'm an invisible saint praying on your rooftop. Let us have broken coffee in Paradise. Let us put the coated tar to our lips in order to flood the morning body along with the fog of the Maghreb. May the God of Matthieu be aroused observing these brushes of delirium at the entrance of my liberated entrails. I do not hide my satisfaction. In fact, I announce it.

# Five

*Par la foi, la libération est aisément obtenue.*
Through faith, liberation is easily obtained.

—BARDO THÖDOL, TIBETAN BOOK OF THE DEAD

# The Bardo of the Moment
of Death

THAT NIGHT IN THE DREAM, Shams is lying in my arms in bed. I keep asking if this is real. He looks up at me but is not responsive. I wake myself up out of fear.

I am pungent this morning. Putrid. Last night's burnt onions, cumin, hard-boiled eggs and french fries are already releasing their poisons. My stomach is a sulfuric mess—what rot. Like flies, he is attracted to my scent.

I rarely bathe now. It causes countless social problems. They let me shower at the men's public bath because women only have the hammam. This devours me both as woman and woman kept. I have pimples everywhere but he loves me and I am saved—no matter for how long.

*"J'en ai vraiment mare de cette vie de chien—qu'est ce que tu en dis? En général je me sens comme un être affreux, ravagé, corps et esprit. J'entends, j'entends la Totale!"* wails Matthieu. I'm really sick of this dog life—what do you say? These days I feel like an awful, ravaged person. Body and mind. I hear, I hear the Absolute. "And I still can't understand how a woman like you could care about me, stay with me, and desire me even—deep down maybe I'm not all bad, plus I write well. I would offer you ten more crazy years of youth before we made any babies."

"I can no longer be sexual with you," I blurt out in imperfect French.

Matthieu shrugs his shoulders and with a childlike look says, "That's okay, I have no sex drive, anyway. I don't care. I love you."

"Look!" I shout, "I've had it up to here lying in wait like a lunatic in the Middle Atlas smoking your Marquises. I'm with you but I'm not with you! In my heart I'm with someone else, I'm still with Shams!"

Matthieu pauses for some time before countering. In a gentle manner, he says, "I have the impression that our relationship is based on a kind of misunderstanding, or in fact on several misunderstandings. But that doesn't take away my love for you—it remains intact."

The ghosts liberate themselves from the walls, it is soon time to leave. We calm down by smoking kif, drinking opium. He retires. I can do nothing against this desperation. Intoxicate me full time, I beg of you! It is greater than I. This broken heart is a violent release of energy that detonates in the chest and causes a surge unknown to the vast majority. I imprison myself. Disfigure myself. Consume myself. There is nothing left to eat. I don't eat. I am static, well-drugged and well-sentenced to a permanent condition.

Meanwhile, Matthieu lets out a bloodcurdling scream from the next room and I run. He is facing the far window, gesticulating wild. His speech frenetic. Body jerks to one side. Suddenly, he turns around and talks at an invisible person beside me, then another. He is hallucinating people all around him in the room. Morbid visions. Abrupt, he lets out another thundering cry, strikes the air fighting an unknown assailant. Lunges at me but loses his balance and crashes to the floor, trembling. His eyes are open but he does not see. Does not hear. A manic episode. We stop breathing.

# The Clear Lights Seen
# Immediately After Death

IN A STATE OF TERROR. His body has seized up. I freeze inside myself. Crippled while also wanting to run. But I can only kneel before him, and take his foot in my hand. Massage the feet, the fingertips like prayer beads. *La ilaha illallah, La ilaha illallah, La ilaha illallah, La ilaha illallah.* He does not react. And everywhere prayer. The *azan* gives the call and all the day is quartz. *La ilaha illallah, La ilaha illallah.*

"*Je sais que tu n'as jamais rencontré quelqu'un comme moi. Admet le. Admet le,*" he mumbles half-consciously as I put him to bed. I know you've never met anyone like me. Admit it. Admit it.

Matthieu eventually falls asleep. I place him on the mattress, cover him with a blanket and put a wine bottle of water beside the bed. *Al Fatiha.* Heal those who need it. Become more deeply self by removing self. A power progresses through these impulses.

Was his seizure caused by an excess of opium? Had he lied about taking his medication? Was this the clear light?

Next evening when Matthieu finally wakes, he has no memory of the psychotic break. We shower together at the men's public bath. Our tears nothing under the cold water of these final Moroccan ablutions. The end has a scent. It breathes through us. We lose ourselves in impossible thoughts, oncoming shrouds of rain, necessary testing grounds.

"It's like I imagined something happened, dreamt it. I'm not sure, Maya. Did I hurt you? Did I harm you in any way?" he asks, stroking my neck under the shower.

"No—but I was ready to run."

"I'm never violent," he says confident, taking me in his arms under the spray. "I see the light now, I'll be fine, Maya. Kiss me."

It took a season in hell to begin a move away from Shams and time with those offering more than I could ever offer in return. These days we move very little, but our travels are great.

# The Bardo of the Experiencing
## of Reality (1)

I FLEE MATTHIEU EARLY one August morning though I don't know that I did it the right way. I became the coward, or perhaps the renunciant.

This is an introduction to my decline. I am cursed now, alone in Ville Nouvelle. The city volume pushes hard against heavy hearing, heavy thought. Hold the robes! Perhaps there is a need for ceremony in all this. Humility. Grace. Ritual. I take all these things and separate myself while equally absorbed by the crowd. An extroverted introvert attempting the Great Memory.

One of the songs that the West African ancestors brought through the wretched Middle Passage to enslavement in the Caribbean was *La Alla LaLa*. A clear prayer all the way to beloved Wadadli/Antigua, up to beloved Tiohtià:ke/ Montréal and now back to the beloved Source. The Great

Memory. Astonishment at the familiar. The book and the Mysteries. Ask Shams, he initiated me, though neither of us knew it. *La ilaha illallah.*

The men here would not hurt me, though their crotches move involuntarily at my passing. I know they are my brothers, but I have not walked by myself in some time. I buy a brass teapot from a shopkeeper named Husayn whose hand grazes my breast twice, mid-sentence. He has a bright round face and a black turban from which dark reddish hair peeks out. He peers at me over his half-moon glasses.

"Are you married?" he inquires, palming his generous beard.

"Are you?" I retort.

We both laugh uncomfortably, neither of us answering. He vanishes into a back room and emerges with a tiny silver hamsa. The Hand of Fatima. Mark of protection. Eye of conscience.

"The five fingers on this Hand of Fatima represent the People of the Cloak, *Ahl al-Bayt*: Hazreti Muhammad '*alayhi s-salām*, Imam Ali, Hassan, Husayn and Fatima, the shining one. *Inshallah* you had good encounters with us here in the land of God."

With these words he places the hand in my hand. It is intricate silver with a glass blue eye staring up central like a full moon that follows you at night in a recurring dream. I disappear inside all those who had come before.

The paradox inherent in travel, the response system, the gall, the privilege, the gifts, the assaults and accounting. Prayer and disrespect side by side. My presence here is not real, but imagined, created with cash and abandon and a desire for all that has been lost.

I'm weak and nearing the end now. Carrying this weight since the disappearance of Shams. I want to be logical but it is difficult. All things repressed are surfacing. Moment of death, the death of love. I go on living despite myself. I do not want to make connections. My heart is bursting. I may die of fright at the awareness of my own condition. If I ever saw Shams again, all my features would fall. Fall into a slow *zikr*, the *zikr* of no end.

# The Bardo of the Experiencing of Reality (2)

THEY'VE SPLIT MY BODY ALL over the pavement. They are kicking my dust all over the place. The Seeing quickly abandon me. Even Shams left me for a hollow reed and a country. I hope they are both good lovers for him.

There is no remedy for this pain. It is not getting easier to accept. A loss grips the throat, crushes the inside of the head, pounds at the chest. A dense pain in the constant belly, loins up. I am on my knees, bloodied. Crawling the medina blind, touching walls to find my place, mouth open to receive racism and flies with more courage than I. Words are cold coming out of my mouth. I have lost the way to my mouth.

What I need is an exorcism, I am beyond simple prayer now. Presently mad. Non-functional, antisocial, in hibernation. Plagued with memories of Shams and abandonment. In need of cigarettes and water but too frightened of the species to go out and get some. What is this abyss? Even the wind will not take it. From whom did I inherit this? What African ancestry wastes so much on tears?

Doors pounding in this hotel are too loud. I search for errors in the tiling. I hit my knee on the table reaching for an itch. There is no sleep, only cockroaches. Last night one ends up on its back, immobile. I give it my pencil to grip and send it back to the great Outdoors. Madness. A reminder. The call to prayer is awful in this town. High pitched and uninviting like Sirens in the city. May the sound of Sirens be far away from you. They can throw curses like I can throw skin. Androgynous even, you'll never see us coming.

Is this how to be perfectly supple and pliable in the hands of Truth? Not stiff like a corpse, they tell me. I remember now. There is no way to forget.

This peeling of paper-thin skin is a violent acceptance of the past, adherence to the moment. There's nothing left to lose, nowhere left to turn, and so I turn myself in/to You. From a knot in the plexus, a lump of imagination, a lesson in vulnerability. This pain, an energy pattern. The transit of Saturn. The whole work of the whole heart. The whole story witnessed from just beyond the stage.

I held onto Shams tight. To let go was to die. But Shams let go instead, and I died. Posthumously, I'll tell all.

# The After-Death World

IN THE DREAM, WE ARE AT the edge of a large field of rolling hills near the sea. The landscape is bathed in a muted silver. There is a warm, pleasing wind across the open expanse. An eerie twilight before the rise when moon still cuts a pearl on the water. A few people are in conversation or walking around aimlessly in the distance.

Sitting beside me is the man who will become my *semazenbashi*. He is the observer, the one who watches. I would later learn to fast and cross the harbour by boat every week to study with him. When you long for something lost, when you don't know where to turn, whirling is logical.

In the dream, the observer speaks without speaking. His lips do not move but the message is clear. "Die before you die," says a voice that is not his.

The people around us were being transformed. Some had died of old age or in their sleep, some from accidents, war injuries or disease. One man was completely deformed. His jaw was wide open, bleeding, there was no skin, and his face was covered in red pustules. Some bodies were solid, others transparent. Some bodies were missing limbs, one was headless.

We were in the land of the dead where the ones who do not yet realize they have died must die again. Once acceptance of death occurs, the transparencies and deformities are replaced with solidity. The person is whole again, organic, tranquil, happy and briefly unlimited.

Pray the Truth comes quickly for us all. Though I have partial sight, it will take millennia for this eclipse to fully pass.

# The Process of Rebirth

TODAY, DESPAIR TAKES a step back with the arrival of Matthieu in Fes to wish me goodbye. He had sobered up, turned ascetic the last five days without me. His florid cheeks and freshly shaven head pleased me. His presence kept the sorrow at bay. My thermal south briefly warmed in the hands of this poet. Being in love takes on new meaning. Without an object, what does one do with the feeling? Perhaps in the middle of *that* ocean, with no land in sight, the only choice is surrender, the giving away.

*"Il y a des moments où ça fait peur et tu sais comme mon équilibre mental est fragile."* There are times when it's scary and you know how my mental state is fragile, says Matthieu.

I arrived in parts but managed to put myself together with water, khubz, modest clothing, resin, bitter wine, carnal endeavours and Matthieu, the gift from God.

"And your vow of chastity?" I ask.

"Chasti-what?" he replies, stroking my sex.

*"Nous vivons beaucoup de choses en peu de temps,"* he whispers in my ear. We are living many things in a short time. "Kiss me Maya, it's my birthday." He is twenty-one.

Shams is nothing but poetry now. We were briefly immortal, then both guilty. I must take responsibility for myself.

I hear through the mouths of others that Shams is well. Not long after we had split in Paris, news arrived that he had been spotted in Istanbul and had possibly taken a wife. Take refuge, leave refuge. I failed to keep the company of my beloved. But I will never fail Love. One Truth is hidden inside all the events of the world. And now, there is no separation from the company of Secrets. It was the company sought all along.

I came to the door of Love but you turned me away. So this one became a dervish in the axis of the heart. Now there is a dervish at the door, to whom no one can refuse entry.

*Astaghfirullah*

## AUTHOR'S NOTES

The soundtracks for this text are Yakaza Ensemble's *Amak-i Hayal*, Alice Coltrane's *Reflection on Creation and Space* and Charlie Parker's *Confirmation: The Best of the Verve Years*.

An excerpt of *Book of Wings* appears in the anthology *Changing the Face of Canadian Literature* (Guernica Editions) and the poem "Cooked" appears in *Nouveau Griot* by Tanya Evanson (Frontenac House).

With thanks to Dimitri Nasrallah and Kaie Kellough for their literary third eye; Simon Dardick for the full circle; Isabelle Savard and Shirin Sacek for linguistic support; J who threw me out; L who took me in; Sherif Baba Çatalkaya, Cem Aydoğdu and Raqib Brian Burke who guided me; Mom, Dad and Melissa for eternal love; and Temmuz Arşiray—beloved husband and muse—for being my true companion in the end. Give thanks.

ESPLANADE
*Books*

THE FICTION IMPRINT AT VÉHICULE PRESS

*A House by the Sea* : A novel by Sikeena Karmali
*A Short Journey by Car* : Stories by Liam Durcan
*Seventeen Tomatoes : Tales from Kashmir* : Stories by Jaspreet Singh
*Garbage Head* : A novel by Christopher Willard
*The Rent Collector* : A novel by B. Glen Rotchin
*Dead Man's Float* : A novel by Nicholas Maes
*Optique* : Stories by Clayton Bailey
*Out of Cleveland* : Stories by Lolette Kuby
*Pardon Our Monsters* : Stories by Andrew Hood
*Chef* : A novel by Jaspreet Singh
*Orfeo* : A novel by Hans-Jürgen Greif
[Translated from the French by Fred A. Reed]
*Anna's Shadow* : A novel by David Manicom
*Sundre* : A novel by Christopher Willard
*Animals* : A novel by Don LePan
*Writing Personals* : A novel by Lolette Kuby
*Niko* : A novel by Dimitri Nasrallah
*Stopping for Strangers* : Stories by Daniel Griffin
*The Love Monster* : A novel by Missy Marston
*A Message for the Emperor* : A novel by Mark Frutkin
*New Tab* : A novel by Guillaume Morissette
*Swing in the House* : Stories by Anita Anand
*Breathing Lessons* : A novel by Andy Sinclair
*Ex-Yu* : Stories by Josip Novakovich

*The Goddess of Fireflies* : A novel by Geneviève Pettersen
[Translated from the French by Neil Smith]
*All That Sang* : A novella by Lydia Perović
*Hungary-Hollywood Express* : A novel by Éric Plamondon
[Translated from the French by Dimitri Nasrallah]
*English is Not a Magic Language* : A novel by Jacques Poulin
[Translated from the French by Sheila Fischman]
*Tumbleweed* : Stories by Josip Novakovich
*A Three-Tiered Pastel Dream* : Stories by Lesley Trites
*Sun of a Distant Land* : A novel by David Bouchet
[Translated from the French by Claire Holden Rothman]
*The Original Face* : A novel by Guillaume Morissette
*The Bleeds* : A novel by Dimitri Nasrallah
*Nirliit* : A novel by Juliana Léveillé-Trudel
[Translated from the French by Anita Anand]
*The Deserters* : A novel by Pamela Mulloy
*Mayonnaise* : A novel by Éric Plamondon
[Translated from the French by Dimitri Nasrallah]
*The Teardown* : A novel by David Homel
*Aphelia* : A novel by Mikella Nicol
[Translated from the French by Lesley Trites]
*Dominoes at the Crossroads* : Stories by Kaie Kellough
*Book of Wings* : A novel by Tawhida Tanya Evanson